Prodigal Son

(Lost Son) and a Father's Love

Roger Roberge Rainville

Prodigal Son
A Lost Son and a Father's Love

Author: Roger Roberge Rainville

ISBN 978-1-935018-98-8

Interior Design: Leo Ward
Cover Design: Randall Eric Johnson

Published by:
Discipleship Publishing
A Division of: The International Localization Network
randy2905@gmail.com
ILNcenter.com

-|-

Acknowledgements

Writing Expertise

Thanks to Dr. Amy Kimmel for her contribution to this work (teacher at Canisius High School, Buffalo New York). Her help, support, and guidance proved to be invaluable in the completion of this project. (Shalom!)

The Artwork

Thanks to Diane Noody, (Hamburg, New York) an accomplished artist, for her original renderings of various scenes in the story.

Contents

Introduction

One of the most interesting stories Jesus told as recorded in the Word of God is the one about the "Prodigal (Lost) Son." (Luke 15:11-32) To me, it has all of the dynamics of any average family: a parent's love for his children, family loyalty, sibling character differences, maintaining strong ties to home and land and not abandoning those you love. Also, as it so often happens in families, common unpleasant events that break up solid families. In this story, one of the sons wants to leave home to go off to some strange and foreign country – where people do not practice the same beliefs and do not have the same moral laws of conduct as our young adventurer is used to. As a young Hebrew man, there were certain things he should have never exposed himself to - but he did.

Just looking at our own society today, it is very easy to see where a young person can end up if he or she chooses to live in a way that is worldly and put aside or disregard all the good things learned while growing up as taught by parents. In life, everyone chooses to "live" or "die" spiritually. In this story, our young man experienced the good life he had before his adventure, then came his spiritual death, and his torturous journey back home - back to his father.

Jesus did not say where the young man was from, nor give any other details than those found in Luke chapter 15. In reading the famous story, the following questions arose in my mind:

What was the young man's name? What were his parent's name, his brother's name? Did he have sisters, and if so, what were their names? How much inheritance money did he walk away with? What "foreign" country did he travel to, and how far from home was he? Where did he stay? Exactly what sort of people and activities was he involved with? What eventually happened to all of his money? After his state of destitution when the famine hit, what happened? How did he make it back home without money, food, and no shoes? How long did it take him to get back home? What happened after his father came to meet him as he was nearing home?

Although mostly fiction, the events described in this work will offer you some answers and provide insight into how everything could have unfolded for this adventurous young man who made some bad choices and found out soon enough that he was wrong and needed to make things right between him and God, and then, between him and his father.

Prodigal Son Characters

Amiel *(Of the Lord's people)* .... the father

Amon *(faithful)* .... oldest son

Bo *(swift and strong)*...younger son

Chaver *(friend)*.. Bo's donkey

Bluma *(flower)*..temptress

Amed .... innkeeper

Jamal ....Amed's wife's uncle (a businessman)

Fadil *(generous)* ....Amed's cousin

Sabah *(sunshine)*..Bo's maid

Abdul *(servant)*..foreman

Kasib *(provider)* .... manager

Ella *(bright)* .... plant worker

Jamila *(beautiful)*...plant worker

Sophia.. inn servant

Mia.. inn servant

Metuka *(sweetheart)* .... poor little girl

Monetary Values in Jesus' Days

The following will be useful to figure the cost of things as you read keeping in mind that *20 cents a day* was an average day's wage, consider the following equivalencies:

A talent = $2,000

A mina = 1/60 of a talent or $35.00

A Jewish shekel = 1/50 of a mina or 65 cents

A Syrian stater = 50 cents

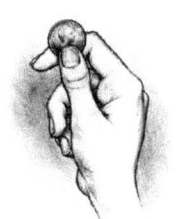

A Roman *denarius = 20 cents

A roman assirion = 1 cent

A roman quadrant = ⅛ of a cent

A Jewish prutah/perutah or lepton = ¼ cent

The latter coin was the amount of the "*widow's mite*" mentioned in one of Jesus' story about the *Widow's Two Mites*.

(2 mites = about two-thirds of a cent)

The Parable of The Prodigal Son

This story begins with a well-to-do family who lives on the outskirts of the city of Nazareth who has an estate, servants and field hands. It's about a man named Amiel and his two sons. He loves both sons equally. They both take care of his assets: overseeing the lands, the stock and managing the hired hands. Both sons have an equal share in their father's estate. The older son Amon, age twenty-five, is resigned to staying with his father, but the younger son, Bo, twenty-one, on the other hand, wants to spread his wings and go it alone, away from home, to a foreign country to find fun and adventure in his *Utopia!* His destination is not mentioned, but for the sake of reference, let's say he leaves the Nazareth area for Beirut in Lebanon (Ancient name – Biruta) (over 100 miles away), a metropolis at the time, on the coast of the Mediterranean Sea. He needs his part of the inheritance so that he can leave and fulfill the desires of his heart.

Amon, his older brother, is married and has a boy four years old and a daughter a little over two years of age. He and his family live on part of the estate in a modest but nice house. Bo still lives with his father, one older sister, Ana, and a younger sister named Ruth. His mother, Sarah, passed away a few years back.

Utopia – a make believe place where everything is blissful

Bo

Bo's character is different from that of his older brother Amon. Amon is sensible and mature while Bo is impulsive and often does things that get him into a bit of trouble, whether it be in speech or action. He often falls into that problem of "engaging mouth before brain" - saying things carelessly without thinking first.

As for some of his actions, again, he does things he regrets doing. One event that will prove to be a mistake, one done without much planning, is leaving home to go to a foreign country – a five day journey! There is an adventurous side to Bo. This will be a good test to see how well he can manage on his own!

His older Amon had chastised him at times as most older and sensible brothers do, not so much for putting Bo down, but for the purpose of watching out for him so that he learns to be more careful with his words and actions. That's a big brother's job, watching out for the younger.

Bo also has talents. He is extremely good at shearing sheep. He is very proud of this. He does so faster and better than anyone around, even Amon. Amon knows this and praises him for it; he is not jealous of Bo's talents. Again, Amon's maturity stands out that way, also showing that he is a humble individual. Bo is also very smart in managing the help and organizing the tasks to be done. He brings wool and produce to the markets in the town of Nazareth for the local vendors as well as for the merchants passing through that take them to the outlying towns and villages.

He is tall and handsome, at least six feet tall. Also, he's strong and fast as his name says. He has a very good nature about him and would give anyone the shirt off his back. He isn't spoiled, just adventurous, and has a need to try new and different things. Amon is sensible and quiet in character, but Bo has a "fire" in him; a bit wild, a bit of a restless soul.

Speaking of "fire," he once challenged one of the biggest and toughest young men in the area by the name of Jesse for insulting the older sister Ana. He went to confront this thug, and demanded that he apologize to his sister and his father Amiel. He refused and struck Bo on the jaw. Bo went down, but grabbed a handful of dirt without Jesse knowing it, rose up, approached him and threw the dirt in his eyes. This made him an easy target. Bo rounded behind him, swept his feet with a strong kick to the back of both knees, Jesse came crashing down, slamming his body to the ground which knocked the wind out of him. At the same time, his head hit the ground and nearly rendered him unconscious. Jesse was now dazed and had no fight in him. Bo turned him over onto his stomach, got on top of him and began putting his face in the dirt.

Bo yelled:
"Do you yield?! Will you apologize to my sister and my father for the insults?!

Jesse yielded and said:
"Yes! I yield, and I will apologize to them. I promise!"

The next day, he made his way to Bo's father's house and made sincere apologies. He also apologized to Bo for hitting him. Bo hesitated, but at the prodding of Amon, he accepted.

Amon told Bo:
"It's better to make friends then to make enemies."

The matter was behind them and Jesse never again dared cross the line with Bo's sister or any other young lady in the area. It would seem that Jesse was intelligent enough to realize that there are consequences to certain actions, and that repeating them is not a good thing.

Bo Influenced To Travel

He loves his family. He doesn't mean to hurt anyone's feelings or abandon them by not being there to help run the estate. He let his imagination run wild after speaking with a couple of his friends in town who had gone to Beirut, Lebanon where they had spent a month of wild living. They told Bo all about the crazy and wild times they had with regards to living it up, having fun, drinking and being in the company of women who know how to make a man feel good. Not all good boys who hear or find out about these sorts of things get attracted to it, but, Bo did. He got the urge. He wanted to experience what his friends had told him instead of settling down, getting married, having kids and getting on with regular day to day mundane activities like he was doing on his father's estate.

After thinking a while about going to a big city and taking in some of those pleasures, the urge to go out and experience more of life outside the confines of his day-in and day-out routines, is very strong. He just has this need to satisfy his curiosity, to see new and different sights, and take in as much of life as he can.

He thinks to himself:

"If I don't do this now, I'll never know those experiences. It will always be in the back of my mind that I had the chance to do it and failed to follow my heart."

Can I Have My Money?

Bo's mind is fully made up that he will do this. His quick plans are set, and the next thing he needs is money – his inheritance. For this, he has to speak to Amiel, his father. He feels somewhat anxious to spring this kind of news on him, knowing that his father is somewhat on in years. Leaving means that he may never see his him alive again. That bothers him, but he feels he needs to do this, to get it out of his system.

He sets a time when his father is relaxed and approaches him, saying:

"Father, it is true that I have an inheritance coming to me, correct?"

His father replies:

"Yes son, between you and Amon, what is mine is yours. You know that."

He then tells his father what he has his mind and heart set on doing, and that he needs his share of that inheritance now. This does not please Amiel. It was unheard of for a son to do what was presented him by his own son. His father is cut to the heart and pleads for him to reconsider his plans! Bo assures him that he has no intention of changing his mind.

After much discussion and pleading for his son not to do this, Amiel can see it is no use in trying to deter him. He finally agrees, but very reluctantly. He gives Bo his rightful share of the inheritance.

How Much Money Did Bo Inherit?

Jesus did not state how much he walked away with, but it had to have been a considerable sum, for his father was fairly well-to-do.

For the sake of reference, let's say it was 1,000 dollars, enough to last him nearly fourteen years if he was careful with his spending, keeping in mind that 20 cents was an average day's pay.

A shekel was equaled to 65 cents - A stater was equaled to 50 cents.

A denarius equaled 20 cents (a day's wage). $1,000 dollars divided by 20 cents equaled 5,000 days' worth of wages or about thirteen and a half year - living conservatively.

Imagine leaving home with that kind of money in your pocket going out to look for fun and happy, carefree times. Also imagine some of the ramifications that go along with it. First of all, shouldn't he be worrying someone might find out he is carrying a bag of money with a small fortune in it? How about where to put it when he is out carousing?

He certainly couldn't carry it around with him! What if he got drunk, passed out and someone discovered the bag…. GONE! It could happen that quickly! He will have to devise a plan to safeguard his money so the entire fortune is never taken. A few ideas come to mind. He will work those ideas out in his mind as he walks, and implement them when the time comes.

We know that in Jesus' account, the young man lived it up, but it does not state for how long. We can only speculate based on what an average "foolish" young man leaving home with a small fortune tied to his body might end up doing. Most young men leaving the nest to go miles from home to "find themselves," usually come up with that idea on a whim! This young man was a nice enough lad but lacked any insight as to what could go wrong. He probably didn't have any well thought out plans before he left. In his mind, he wanted to experience what he'd heard other young men talk about. Sound familiar?

He had one thought in mind:
"Let the good times roll!"

A Dad's Advice

Like any good, loving father, Amiel tries to reason with Bo and dissuade him from doing what he has his mind set on. Bo is firm in his decision. Amiel wants him to consider certain things before he leaves the following morning. He asks him questions and counsels him. Amiel begins the conversation.

HE ASKS BO:

"Everyone needs a place to live. Where will you stay son?"

Bo:
"I will be fine father. I will find adequate lodging. I promise. Please don't worry about that."

Amiel:
"Make sure you eat well. Who's going to cook for you? The maids won't be there nor any of the servants to prepare you meals."

Bo:
"I assure you I will not starve. I will be wise with the money you gave me and will take good care of myself."

Amiel:
"Take care of who you meet and who you trust! Watch out for false friends! That's very important. And, be very careful of the women you encounter! Know that all women are not as your mother was or sisters are. Some can be charming and lure you into things you must not do! Do not be led astray!"

Bo:
"Father, I know that and I promise I will be very careful of the company I keep. And, I know enough about women to know that they

can be very seductive. I promise I will honor and keep your advice close to my heart."

Amiel is concerned about the money Bo will be carrying.

Amiel says:
"Be careful how you spend your money – budget well so that it will last. Invest some and make it work for you so you can draw dividends."

Bo:
"I've learned much from you and money matters. I promise I will be careful and invest some of the money."

Amiel:
"Also, son, never ever tell anyone, I mean NO ONE, about your wealth! Trust no one! Only God! "

Bo:
"I will trust no one, only God. And, I'll tell no one about my money, I promise."

Amiel wants to make sure Bo will never forget who he is.

Amiel says:
"Son, remember where you are going, the people there do not live according to the laws of Moses as we do and are not descendants of our forefathers; Abraham, Isaac and Jacob. Never forget where you came from, who you are, and who you must serve! You will see many enticements that might get you to turn away from your heritage, but you must resist with all that is within you so as to retain all that your mother and I have taught you! Be a man of integrity. Be wise in all your ways, for the world in which you're going into can destroy you very quickly if you do not seek God's wisdom and follow His ways."

Bo:

"Father, I will do my very best to honor both our God and you and to keep the Sabbath holy as is the custom of our people."

Amiel:

"Very well Bo. Keep all that we talked about in your heart and do not forget your promises to me. Although I release you reluctantly, I give you my blessing and wish you God's speed. Be safe and prosper. And Bo, always remember that I love you very much – more than life itself!"

Bo:

"Father, I love you too and always will. I will not forget you. I will think of you and the rest of the family every day."

With all that said, Bo hugs his father and Amiel holds onto Bo as tight as he can, almost as though he can't let him go.

BO PREPARES TO LEAVE

It is now Monday morning. Bo gets up to gather what he's going to take on his trip. He doesn't want to travel too heavy. He puts together a couple of bags of clothes, one bag for a couple of good tunics or robes, and another for a few items of older clothing for work. In a third bag, he has three blankets, some food and drinks (water and wine) for several days. In a special bag of religious items for worship, he includes; a prayer scroll, two candles, two loaves of challah bread that represent manna, and a cup for the wine. He also has two separate bags to hold his money; a small one that he will carry in his waistband and a larger one, well hidden under his clothes. One more thing, he needs a donkey to carry his belongings. His father gives him a one year old donkey that Bo helped birth and named him, Chaver.

One good thing Bo did before leaving, he went to a money changer and changed some of the minas for smaller denominations so that he could better function in market place, inns, and other places where he might need to bed down or eat. He broke it down this way;

28 minas at $35 each came to $980

30 shekels at 65 cents each came to $19.50

A few staters at 50 cent, several denarius worth 20 cents each and, some assirions worth 1 cent each and, prutahs worth a quarter of a cent each.

He straps the twenty-eight minas ($35 each) to his body in the larger money bag and tucks it under his clothes. He has a very good reason for having separated the money that way. If it should happen that there be robbers along the way, he would hand over the smaller bag of money in the sash around his waist. Whatever funds he would need to spend along his trip, he would draw from that smaller purse. He doesn't want to ever expose the small fortune hidden under his clothes.

THE GOOD-BYES

It is now midday. Amiel helps Bo load his belongings onto the donkey.

Amiel wants to try one more time to dissuade Bo from going and says:
"Bo, will you not reconsider this and not leave us?"

Bo responds:
"Father, I know this hurts you, seeing me go. I'm so sorry for hurting you. I really am. I don't mean too. But, I must do this for myself. The urge is strong, and if I don't do this now, it would only haunt me. I would always have this thing hanging over me; that I had the chance to go but stayed back because others thought they knew what was best for me. What's best for me is to go. I hope it goes well. If it doesn't, I will know it in time. But at least, I will have tried. I need to do this!"

Amiel says:
"I understand son. I want you to know, although you may find a new home away from here, remember that this will always be your home... always!"

Bo answers his father:

Yes…this will always be my home. I can't forget that."

Amiel kisses and hugs Bo tightly and wishes him "God's speed." He then steps aside and allows Amon and his sisters to say good-bye and wish him a good journey.

Although Amon still resents his little brother's decision, he hugs Bo as he gets ready to leave. In Amon's mind, Bo is abandoning his family to go out and live it up while he stays behind to make sure his aging father has a family member to watch over his affairs, to keep everything secure, and to ensure that the family business continues. Still ... there is that brotherly love deep inside that tugs at his heartstrings because they are close as brothers. For Amon too, this will leave a hole in his heart at his brothers departure. Amon will miss him terribly.

He says to Bo:
"You know how much I disapprove of this! But, I want you to know that I will miss you. Now then, don't forget what your father said to you, and don't do anything stupid! Your big brother won't be there to watch over you. Take care and be safe."

Bo responds:
"I will take car and be safe. And, thanks for being my big brother. I love you and will not forget you."

It's time to leave. He slings a small sack over one shoulder, grabs the harness to lead Chavier, turns and says one last "good-bye" to everyone, and begins his journey. Everyone from the house is outside and watches as Bo makes his way down the road. Ana and Ruth weep bitterly.

They run after him and each one holds one of his arms and walks a little ways down the road, just to be with him a little longer. They eventually let him go. They kiss his cheek, turn from him and head back toward the house in tears.

Amiel stands fast as his boy walks away. His eyes well up and his heart breaks! He and his family watch Bo go until the sight of him fades to nothing. With tears rolling down Amiel's cheeks, there is such a heaviness his heart, and a great sense of loss, almost as if a loved one had just died!

He figures his son will be gone for good, never to return, that he'd probably get married, settle down somewhere else, and that they would never see each other again. There is now an empty hole in his heart and nothing can fill it or heal it, except, seeing his son return to him.

Amon also waits till he's completely out of sight. As he turns to go in the house, he pauses, and takes one more look in the direction Bo went. He stays there a while and lets memories of his brother run through his mind, memories that are special. He remembers when they were children playing in the yard and running through fields. He remembers the many family gatherings and times when he had to rescue him from some bullies. His eyes fill with tears. He prays that God will keep him safe and bestow blessings on him. Although Bo has gone out of view, Amon raises his hand high and waves it - as a last good-bye. He turns around and joins the rest of the family at the dinner table. Everyone at the table is very quiet. Amiel doesn't stay there long. He eats very little, gets up, goes to his chamber and closes the door.

Everyone knows that he went to morn Bo's absence, privately.

Day One of The Journey—Camping Out

Now on the road to that foreign land with different people, languages, customs and lifestyles, Bo is heading for experiences he never dreamed of. His donkey is fully loaded. His fortune is secured under his garment in a sac. He also has that string-tied bag slung over his shoulder containing a prayer scroll and other items for worship. He looks back toward his home before it goes completely out of sight, knowing that there would always be that something special inside his heart connected to that house and land. It's just a natural thing. His entire life so far has been spent there. He will miss the familiar voices of his father, sisters and brother. He will sorely miss his father's presence in his life; the advice and loving words a father speaks to his son. He will also miss the servants and hired hands.

Call it sentimental attachments or part of belonging, but a person holds on to certain things in this world; some things cannot be shaken off. Bo comes to the top of another hill. He is able to faintly see his house. He takes one last look at his father's place, then turns and heads north with the midday sun warming him. His journey will take him through several larger towns such as Cana, Ptolamais (Acco), Tyre, Sicho, and finally, to Beirut. He would like to cover at least twenty plus miles a day.

As the day progresses, he comes to a point where he feels a need to rest a while before going further. As he sits in a shaded area, passers-by can't help but look at him, thinking:

"What is this young man doing out here alone with all that baggage?"

Also, he gets looks from a few shady characters who eye his belongings.

He sees them looking at him. He looks away quickly, a bit shyly, with a certain degree of discomfort on his face as if to say:

"I don't want any trouble. Leave me alone!"

He just has that look of a guy out of place. His body language, the way he looks at things that are new to him with that "new guy" grin on his face, or perhaps staring a little too long at a beautiful woman who passes by. Something about him says that he is "out-of-place."

He soon realizes some of these things about himself and puts on his "game-face." He realizes that he isn't home anymore with people he knows. His entire being senses that the presence of strangers makes him feel a little uneasy. It's not insecurity, just uncertainty. When one is out in the world, there is this certain unwritten code of conduct that one should adopt; be on guard and be very aware of your surroundings.

His father's words come back to him where he said:

"Trust no one, Only God!"

Thus the "game-face," to look the part of a man you shouldn't bother, to keep your distance, or else!

THE CAMP

The sun is slowly slipping below the western horizon and night will soon be upon him. He has traveled about seventeen miles. Bo sees a tree a fair distance from the road that will serve as a good canopy. He makes his way there and figures it will do for the night. He would much more prefer sleeping in an inn or in a shulgi (rest station,) but he hasn't come upon any so far. A good second choice would be a shelter or a barn. Neither is available, and he has to bed down.

Now then, being used to lying down in his own bed when the day is through, how does he make the adjustment from a nice soft bed in a cozy home, to the hard ground, a cool or cold night and the possibility of being mugged. He ties off Chaver, unloads his belongings and sets them near where he is going to sleep. He makes as comfortable a bed as he can with his blankets. He keeps the money bag with the fortune strapped to him hidden under his cloak. He doesn't want to separate it from him. It's secure!

He settles in, lying on his back, wrapping himself in a nice warm wool blanket his mom made him before she died. Just doing that reminds him of home and strikes a tender chord in his heart! He's only been gone eight hours, yet... he misses home. Strange, isn't it? His sleep is broken by every strange sound he hears. He sits up and looks around to see if anyone has come near his belongings to steal them. So tired, he finally drifts off to sleep.

Day Two—Trouble Strikes

As soon as the first ray of sunlight hits his face from the east, he opens his eyes and quickly realizes where he is and how strange a feeling it is to wake up in a strange place without the usual morning greetings:

"Good morning Bo! How are you? Can I make you some breakfast, son?"

Another thing that strikes him is the stench of animal waste his donkey had produced during the night as he slept. Welcome to the real world Bo! It is sort of a sign of things to come. Think of it, the first day away, and the first thing he experiences as he wakes up is the stench of Chaver's waste. Do you think he had a good night's sleep his first night out? I would think not. As a matter of fact, it gets worse for him.

He goes to a stream about a hundred yards away to wash his face, hands and arms, and rinse his mouth. He turns around and sees a couple of young hooligans run off with some of his belongings. He yells for them to stop and drop the goods, but they laugh as they run like the wind. He runs back to see what they took and notes that a bag of his clothes is gone! And ... oh no!!! The blanket his mother made, that's gone too!

Furious isn't the word! He could kill them for that! That blanket meant so much to him: it isn't just a blanket, it is part of his mother! He actually weeps. The clothes can be replaced, but mom's blanket, gone forever! That hurts a lot!

He finally resigns himself to the fact that he's going to have to be more cautious and take all precautions to not let this happen again. He'll be all the more careful with regards to his belongings. The world had burned him for the first time and it felt really bad. His father's words hit him once again about *"trusting no one."*

It takes Bo a while to get over the loss of his mother's blanket. After a few minutes, he is more composed, but still, very angry. As he takes inventory again, he notices that a small bag containing the scroll of prayer, two candles, the bread, and the cup for his Sabbath prayer ritual, and a mezuzah, was not taken. Calmer, but still very angry, he goes into one of the other bags that contains food; some bread, olive oil, salt, figs and a skin of water and another of wine. He breaks a chunk of the bread, pours a little oil on it, adds a bit of salt and has his breakfast. Mmm…. not like the food he was used at home. You know: lamb, eggs, home fries, waffles and a nice cup of coffee! [Joke!] Well, maybe not that, but something comparable to our own breakfasts. Actually, what Bo is eating is par for the course. He is used to eating bread, honey cake, cheese and fruits. He loves figs!

As he prepares to continue his trek after an hour break, he begins to gather his things to load up his donkey and keeps looking around to see if he can spot the boys in the area. No luck! Not a soul in sight. As said before, Bo's total destination would be over 100 miles in all. It will take him another four days of walking at a steady pace to get there at a rate of nearly twenty plus miles a day with rest breaks and meals. It will not be a fast-paced walk since the road is very rough and not easy to travel on. He figures he'll take his time getting there so that neither he nor the Chaver will wear out too fast in a single day.

It's near mid-morning. As he makes his way toward Beirut, he notes how dusty the road is. Besides him, others are there with their camels, donkeys and other animals. The dust they kick up as they walk becomes part of the unpleasant nuisances he has to put up with. Wow! So far, not much fun! Ah, but the expectation of what is waiting for him keeps him positive. And so … onward he goes.

He had covered only seventeen miles the first day due to a late start. He has almost 90 more miles to go. Since this is his second day, he wants to push a bit harder so as to cover more miles. Just the walk alone is a brand new experience. He had walked from Nazareth, his hometown, to Jerusalem a couple of times to honor Kind David, as a pilgrimage trip, but this is something else.

The second day starts well enough until about ten miles out, when a storm hits and he is in a wide open area with nowhere to take shelter. This slows his pace quite a bit. The wind is strong, and the rain comes down hard. Still, he keeps walking so that he can cover has many miles as possible before he calls it quits. He keeps going and even passes by a shelter, but wants to make the best of the daylight he has.

He walks about two miles further with the rain and wind beating him down. Finally, he's had enough and when he sees a roadside shelter, he heads for it and takes cover. However, he isn't the only one there. A man, his wife and two very young daughters have taken advantage of the shelter as well. He comes in and is cordial to the couple, smiles at the girls and notices that they are soaked and shivering. He also notices how shabbily they are dressed.

"Poor people," he thinks to himself.

He sees that the parents don't have any extra clothing to put on the girls to keep them warm - nor, any for themselves. He takes pity and goes into one of the bags of clothes. He has a couple of his best coats and two other blankets in it. In the other bag, he has a couple of heavy tunics and a spare pair of sandals.

He pulls out the coats and puts one on the smallest girl:
"Here, little one, you need this more than me."

The girls' father tries to stop him, but Bo says:

"Sir, you must let me do this! It's the right thing to do for these babies."

The man nods as if to say, "Okay." He wraps the little girl with his coat and can see right away how relieved she is to be warmed by both the coat and Bo's generosity. He does the same for the other girl. He feels good that he can take care of them. He remembers his home where he has sisters, one still a teen, and he can relate to her being in need. He'd be so thankful to any stranger offering the kind of charity to his sister that he had just shown to these little girls. And, for the parents, he gives them one of his blankets.

Again! They try to say, *"No!"*

But he insists and says:
"I don't need two blankets. I have a very heavy and good one to keep me warm at night. Please take this one! I insist!"

Reluctantly, but gratefully, they take it and thank Bo. One of the little girls thanks him also.

He says:
"You are most welcome metuka (sweetheart)! I'm happy to be able to help. Be warm! Shalom!"

He turns to go back to his spot in the shelter and smiles. This act of kindness makes him feel good.

He settles in a corner of the shelter with his donkey in eye-sight. He then unwraps some of the food he has and begins to eat. He senses the eyes of the family looking at him and slowly glances their way. As his eyes catch the youngest girl's face, he can see the need. She's hungry. He has a cake of figs that he cut into bite size chunks and motions to her to come and get some. The mother holds her back, but a determined child, who can stop her? She slips her mother's light grip and comes to Bo.

She takes the figs and says:
"Thank you, sir."

Bo gently grabs her arm to hold her there and gives her a loaf of bread to take to her family. He reaches for the skin of water, walks over and gives it to the father.

Before they can say anything, he says:
"Sir, I must do this for you and your wife. I'm sure you would do the same for me. Now, eat and drink! Be fed!"

Once more, as Bo turns, he smiles and says to himself:
"You're a good man Bo! This kindness will surely return to you."

The family and our young traveler stay there until the rain stops. By that time, it is six o'clock in the evening. He thinks about heading out to walk for a couple of hours more but then decides that two more hours won't make that much of a difference. He isn't in any real hurry. Beirut will still be there whenever he gets there. He unloads his beast and makes a place where he can sleep. As he sits there, the girls play quietly with a couple of their carved toys. The parents speak with Bo a while about where they're from, where he's from, and where he is going. As he tells them that he is heading to Beirut, the man counsels him by telling him what to lookout for when he gets there. He is about fifteen years older than Bo and has been there. He tells him to keep a safe distance from certain areas and not to trust strangers.

Again, Bo's father's words ring in his head:
"Trust no one!" Only God!"

Although he tells the couple that he left home to go to Beirut, he doesn't say why he is doing so nor does he mention anything about the wealth he has still secured to his body under his cloak. He tells a few lies to make up a good story as to why he left Nazareth to go to that heathen city. He tells them that his father is a merchant and that he is going to meet him and a few other hired hands to escort them back in a caravan of camels and donkeys laden with fine fabrics, silverware items and spices. He tells them that his dad is older and needs him there to lead the caravan. This way, his father can rest as much as possible for the hundred plus miles distance. He also tells them some truth – that he wants to see some of the sights and experience the big city life before they all head back home to Nazareth. They talk for a good while and then retire to their respective spot in the shelter to sleep.

All is well…. and everyone has a restful night.

Day Three

When Bo wakes up, he sees that the family is still sleeping and huddled together. He gets up quietly and begins to load up his donkey. As he is doing that, the older girl gets up and tugs on his tunic so as to not wake up the rest of her family.

She says:
"Here mister! Here's your coat. Thank you very much. It kept me very warm all night!"

The morning is very cool.

He squats down to her height and says in a soft voice:
"No, metuka. You keep it. It's too heavy for my donkey to carry all those coats and blankets. We have a very long way to go. Really! Keep it and be warm, okay? I insist!"

She says:
"Thank you so much, sir! I will take good care it!"

He says:
"I know you will. Tell your sister to keep her coat too and your parents, to keep the blanket, yes? I don't need them. Shalom!"

She says:
"Thank you so much for all that you did. You have no idea how much it means to us. Thank you! Thank you! Thank you! And God bless you!"

He replies:
"God bless you, too, and keep you and your family safe and warm as you travel."

She puts her arms around his neck, kisses his cheek and hugs him, then, walks back to her family. Her father, lying with his face to the wall, heard the little conversation and just smiles – for both, his little girl thanking Bo and for the kind and sweet words he had for his daughter. He wants to get up and thank him too, but he knows that what his little girl did was all Bo needed to hear. The father closes his eyes and rests a while longer to give Bo time to leave before getting his family up and moving along to where they are going.

THREE DAYS TO GO

He leads Chaver out from under the shelter and quietly slips away toward his destination. As he walks, he notices that his back has this kink in it. Oh, how he missed his bed! Little by little, as he walks, the tightness in his back subsides.

He thinks to himself:

"Thank God the pain is gone!"

The next three days would be very uncomfortable if it hadn't gone away. As it is, his feet start to ache a bit as the morning wears on. Not too much, but he can definitely feel the soreness.

He thinks to himself again:

"I hope that doesn't become a major problem! I have quite a few more miles to go before I get there!"

He stops at a brook that he sees along the way and goes to soak his feet for relief. He makes sure this time that his beast is very close to him so no one can steal from him again.

He also makes sure he has his walking stick that he can use as a weapon to defend himself. He learned to use one for that very purpose and is very good at it. He and Amon used to practice sparring a few times a week, just to stay sharp. He once dealt with three thieves who came to steal from one of his father's flocks.

He moved like lightning and was very accurate as he delivered the blows with his stick. The word got around among the thieves and would-be thieves in Bo's area.

They said that:

"Bo is someone you do not want encounter should you try to steal from his father's land!"

Along with the split head each thief received, two had broken ribs and one had a broken arm and broken leg. Bo had a "reputation" in his area that kept unsavory types away from him and his family.

Yes, his first day out, he let down his guard and was robbed. It was unlike him to be so careless. This event still bothered him and he was still angry with himself. He vowed that he wouldn't let that happen again.

From then on, he was going to make sure of three things:

[1] He'd keep a closer eye on his belongings,

[2] Keep his walking stick close by for defense and,

[3] Not allow the money bag to be discovered!

Soaking his feet feels really great and he can feel the benefit of that little pause in his journey. As he sits there, his mind wanders back to his home.

He says to himself:

"This is good! No work in the fields, no hollering at the hired hands to get this or that done. No smelly stables to put up with, resting when I want to, no big brother undermining me, and no dad to put me down when I mess up. I'm free to be whatever I want to be and do whatever I want to do, with no one to whom I need to give account to. This is the life I want."

After about a half hour of soaking, he puts on his sandals and begins the journey anew. It is about 11:00AM and he figures he will walk another two hours before taking his next break. The road is busy enough for that time of day; a few individuals going to who knows where, families going to a nearby towns, small caravans with camels and donkeys laden with goods. In fields a distance from the road, Bo can see young men herding sheep. One of the things about the road is that it is rugged and tough to walk on, in some places, very hard to walk on. This makes his pace much slower than he would like it to be. He has to watch his every step!

Another thing he notices is that there are unsavory types either walking by him or hanging around in the villages he passes by. He makes sure he keeps looking over his shoulder so that no one can get too close to him. This becomes a habit as he walks. He walks a ways, comes to a stop, looks around, walks around his beast to make sure all is still secure, that nothing has come loose. While he does this, his head is always tilted downward which makes it seem from a distance that he is looking at his belongings only, but his eyes look at every angle possible to make sure no one is too close. Even when it looks like a stranger might come close to him as he passes by, he creates a safe distance so that he can react if trouble comes. He positions his trusty walking stick in such a way that passers-by feel a bit intimidated by it. This keeps people at bay.

The Dung Pile
Not Funny Now, But Funny Later and, An Intervention

One of the funny things about not looking at the road at all times is that Bo eventually steps into a huge dung dropped by one of the bulls of another traveler. He manages to hit a three inch-deep pile of fresh manure that cakes up throughout his left foot and everywhere on his sandal. Now, what to do? With no stream nearby to wash his foot and sandal, he has to keep walking in that condition until he can come across a brook, a stream or a river. Finally, after a couple of miles, he spots a small stream. He makes his way there and takes care of his needs.

While he's there, he provides water for Chaver. He takes time for a bite to eat and have a drink himself. He sits down to rest awhile before moving on again. As he's sitting there, he sees three young men (teens) and a young lady arguing with another young man. Suddenly, the three begin to beat up on the lone youth. The beating is getting severe.

He grabs his stick and yells:
"Hey you! Why are you beating this young man so badly!? Stop it!"

One of them responds:
"Mister! Mind your own business! Walk away or you'll be next!"

Bo can see that these are bad characters and will not leave the youth alone. They continue to beat him, and he warns them to stop or he will intervene. They ignore him until he strikes one on the ankle, which makes him stop and writhe in pain. The other two turn to face Bo and make a move toward him. Quick as lightning, he pokes one in the mid-section, which doubles him over and hits the other youth on the side of the knee. He is exact in using his staff. His strikes are meant to hurt a lot, but not do excessive damage.

Now, all three young men are on the ground in pain. Bo tells them that he does not want to hurt them anymore and that they should not treat a person this way.

One youth replies:

"But, he gravely insulted our sister. We wanted to make him pay for it!"

Bo asks the young man who had been beaten if he indeed had done what the others said he'd done.

He answers:

"Yes."

Bo tells him that he needs to apologize and ask forgiveness for his action. The young man agrees.

He turns to the young lady, bows his head, and says:

"I am very sorry for having insulted you and for causing you sorrow. I was wrong. I apologize. Please forgive me!"

She replies:

"I forgive you. But, don't ever again speak to me or any of my sisters the way you did! It was very hurtful and shameful!"

The young man nods his head and backs away to leave. The others thank Bo and agree to let things be. He goes back to sit a while and reflects on what had just happened.

His thoughts are:

"This is not a good world; so many people wanting to hurt each other. One young man's words turned into a beating that could have killed him if I hadn't stepped in! Things should not be this way."

He rests a little while longer then takes to the road again.

Halfway There – And, A Tempting Offer

A fter two and a half days of walking, he feels he's making fair to good progress and is, in fact, half way there. He has walked about fifty-two miles and feels good, not too tired, but senses that the rest of the trip will be challenging. He's determined to do it though. He's still waiting to see all that the city has to offer him. As he makes his way through several of the towns along the road to Beirut, he wants to stay away from the inns or any area where there might be trouble or he might get robbed. He does however stop into a roadside stand where two women are cooking and selling fresh-baked raisin cakes.

It is near sunset, now. Bo has been walking steadily, except for a few pauses to rest, eat, and relieve himself. The latter is particularly tricky. Whenever that need comes up, he has to go off the road with his donkey and into a secluded area with bushes, to be out of eye-shot of anyone passing by. He would never think of leaving Chaver tied off somewhere so that he could take care of personal needs. Where he goes, Chaver goes.

He is already a few miles into Lebanon and comes to the town of Baca. There, he is approached by a lovely young lady named Bluma who takes his breath away. She smells so good and her face is lightly painted (make-up). She speaks to him in a very sweet voice, asking him if he needs a place to stay for the night. She can tell he isn't from that area by the clothes he is wearing. They are a dead give-away. Since he is traveling, she knows he is Israeli and figures has to have money.

She says to him:
"Do you need a place to stay for the night? My brother and I have a house and a cottage on the edge of town just at the end of this street. You could stay in the cottage next to the house for one assirion." (one assirion is equal to a fifth of a day's pay.)"

Mentioning an amount she wanted for the cottage was a way for her to see if he had money and perhaps even find out how much he had.

Bo answers:

"No, I don't need a place to stay. I'm sure I will find shelter further on down the road."

She says:

"You may indeed find shelter along the road, but nothing as comfortable as our cottage. Surely you must have enough money to pay for lodging. All travelers I've seen have money for such an expense. Don't you have one assirion for lodging and food for one night?"

It is very tempting! He thinks about her offer and remembers what his father had told him.

"Trust no one! Only God!"

He also remembers the Proverbs where it warns about painted women. Besides that, although he is young, he has seen some pretty but unscrupulous women in his own town that reminded him that sweet-talking women sometimes have ulterior motives when coming on that way and pretending like they are looking out for a naïve young man's interests. He graciously says "no" and thanks her for the offer.

She tries again to persuade him to go with her to at least check out the accommodations to see if he would not change his mind.

She grabs his arm in a flirtatious way, smiles, and says to him:

"You look so tired. You would be very comfortable there! I could take care of ALL your needs! I would feed you, bring water for you to wash yourself, and take care of your donkey. You would have a nice place to sleep tonight instead of being out ALONE in the cold night."

Bo is even more tempted to take her up on the offer as she presses him again. She is so beautiful and her voice, so sweet ... one that is very hard to resist. Her charms almost win him over. He is able to read between the lines of her statement: "I could take care of all your needs." He knows that means more than food, water and a place to sleep. He had heard stories from his friends about beautiful and seductive young women. His final decision is made when his father's words come back to him about trusting people.

He declines her invitation a second time, thanks her, and keeps going until he makes it a little further than the edge of town. Actually, where he stops isn't too far from where her house is. As was his routine, he pauses a short distance away and walks around to check his beast. As always, he holds his head downward to give the impression that he is only looking at his belongings. This time, he sees the young lady out of the corner of his eye. She is following him, probably, to see if he will settle down somewhere nearby. He then sees her go into a house.

There are a few shelters a little ways from where he encountered her. He moves on a bit further and turns into one of the shelters.

He hears a "still small voice" inside telling him to heed another one of his father's advice ...

His father told Bo:

"Son! Whenever you bed down for a night, hide your money away from you and your belongings and only keep a small amount on you that you can hand over to thieves who might come in the night to rob you!"

THE MISDIRECTION IDEA – HIDING THE MONEY

It is somewhat dark and no one can see clearly inside the shelter from a distance. This is the perfect time to hide the greater part of his inheritance. Bo finds some hay in the shelter. He digs a hole in the ground – not too deep, just enough to put his money in, covers it with a cloth, dirt and hay.

The fact that the town is so close, he doesn't trust anyone, and that the girl has followed him, makes him very suspicious. His father's words stayed with him about, "trusting non one." He only puts in a denarius, a couple of shekels, some assirions and a few quadrants in his waist pouch. That would be a fair haul for any thief should he be caught by surprise and have to hand over any money. Having the money in a safe place, he's all set to make ready for a good night's sleep, or so he thinks!

ANOTHER NIGHT – ANOTHER EPISODE

He unburdens his donkey, sets his goods near him, makes a small fire, and settles down. Once more, he takes out what food he has and eats, drinks a bit of the wine, and rests against the pile of his baggage. Doing that makes it more secure. And always, his walking stick is near him. It is now late evening and he needs sleep. He places a rope with a couple of bells on it between him and his donkey in case anyone tries to sneak up on him in the night. Smart move! His hunch is right about trusting no one!

He lies down and falls asleep. Two men approach the shelter. They come in and make a move toward Bo, and bump into the rope which sets off the alarm. Bo is quick to react! He has his stick in his hands and thrusts it into one of the men's throat, but the second thief gets through, jumps in, and begins to fight with him, which causes Bo to lose his stick. The other regains his composure and comes to the other man's aid.

He pulls out a knife and it holds to Bo's throat, saying:
"Give us your money or die!"

Bo responds…
"I only have a denarius, a couple of shekels, some assirions and a few quadrants! Please don't leave me destitute, please!!! "

Bo is hamming it up with a believable plea for mercy.

One of the men replies…
"We don't care whether you're destitute or not Jewish pig! Give us all you have, right now or we'll cut your throat and take your money anyway!"

Bo complies and gives them the small leather bag he has that contains what he had put into it. The weight of the denarius, the shekels and the assirions makes it feel like there is a good amount. They believe that it is all he has. Due to the darkness, they can't see what else Bo has with him. The fire has died down to just glowing ashes. As they look around as best they can, they only feel the one heavy blanket he has and a couple of bags containing clothes, (one with clean clothes and one with dirty clothes.) They bought the whole "destitute" thing. He is so relieved he hid the inheritance money and having a second bag to give the thieves.

Now then, the one who got hit in the throat isn't happy enough with the money. He figures he owes Bo a little something for the pain he suffered, and still feels. Bo is still down on the ground when the thief kicks him in the face. This leaves him semi-conscious for a while. The two leave quickly and also grab a bag containing clothes. They unknowingly grabbed the bag with the dirty clothes. He thanks God for the advice his father had given him of hiding the money anytime he needed to bed down. Not only that, but he thanks God for the darkness. The thieves got away with very little money, compared to what he actually has, and he gets to keep the bag containing the clean clothes!

After shaking off the wooziness from the beating he had taken, he looks around outside the shelter to make sure they aren't still lurking about. He then goes to the pile of hay to retrieve his money.

He thinks for a moment:
"Had I not heeded my father's warning about the possibility of being robbed, it would all be gone. Praise be to Jehovah!"

He thanks God again and again for being so kind to him. Another thought comes to him. If he hadn't given the two very good coats to the young girls and the blanket to their parents, and the robbers had seen them, they might have thought that he was somewhat well-to-do. The fact that he only had the one old and heavy worn blanket and two small bags of clothes, made it look like he was average and did not have much indeed. He took that as a lesson.

He thinks to himself:
"This is good. Don't be flashy! Don't look like you have anything any-one would want."

MOVE TO ANOTHER SHELTER

He packs up and moves to another location in the cover of night. He goes only about a half mile from where he was and finds an abandoned barn. He quickly ducks inside, unloads his donkey and begins the process of securing his money. It is very dark inside that barn, but there is enough light to see what he needs to do. He digs another hole where he stores the money for the night. There is no straw, but there is a worn out door that has been tossed on the ground. He places it and some other trash over the money. Again, he sets up his rope-and- bell burglar warning system. This time, he sets it near the doorway, the only entrance, which is a fair distance from where he's going to lie down. He's very tired. He makes his bed and lies down. It is now around midnight. Still a bit shaken from the two thieves, he spends the night half awake. He has his walking stick in his hands at the ready even more so, now! He does manage to get a couple of solid hours of sleep, but he still feels tired as he wakes just a little after sunrise. He can't help but wake up. There are roosters in the area, and their crowing reached his ears. He offers up prayers to God for his family and prays for a good day for himself; that the Lord will bless and keep him safe for the remainder of his journey.

Day Four – Getting Close

Since he had given his water to the family a couple of days earlier, he doesn't have any water to wash his face and rinse his mouth, only the wineskin with a fair amount of wine still left in it. He loads his donkey and makes his way down the road hoping to come upon a stream so he can wash and afterward, have his breakfast. He is glad the thieves hadn't taken his food, not that he couldn't buy more, but that he doesn't want to go into his inheritance money to buy anything on his journey. He wants to save the bulk of it for when he gets to Beirut so that he can see how he will spend it and on what. Right now, he wants to hold on to as much of it as he can. Until he gets to Beirut, he has no real idea what is waiting for him, where he will stay, who he will keep company with, and whether or not there will be opportunities to invest some of the money so that it can pay him dividends. If there will be opportunities to invest, the questions is: where and with whom? He remembers his father's words about investing. He knows he'll have to be wise.

Bo is now a little over two-thirds of the way there. He is getting a bit excited knowing that the next day he'll be in Beirut and can start living his dream. He begins walking in hopes he will find a stream where he can wash before eating as is customary for a Jew to do, and to clean up after his meal also. He needs to cover as many miles as he can on this fourth day. It is a pleasant day, mild, with only a slight breeze, which makes the walk even more tolerable. The downside is the terrible condition of the road. It makes traveling much slower than he expected. He thought he'd be much closer to his destination by now.

He looks for a well in the next village where he can wash, then stop and eat before really pushing forward. Finally, in the distance, he sees a small village between Baca and Sidon. As he makes his way in, he goes as quickly as he can to find a well. He asks a young boy where the village well is located. The boy directs him to a place behind an inn. He makes his way there and washes himself. From there, he goes a short way to the edge of the village, and finds a tree under which he can rest and eat.

Before eating, he thanks the Lord for this part of the journey, and the raisin bread he had gotten from the roadside stand in another town. He asks God's blessing for the food and the hands that made it, and begins to eat. He plans on resting for only a short while because he doesn't want to waste any time. He is beginning to feel the long walk and the lack of sound sleep he'd been used to when he was home. On this journey, there are no niceties and the luxury of a nice warm bed. In his earlier days, he had camped out where a flock of sheep ended their grazing, but four days on the road with no "comforts of home" was taking its toll on him and he knew it. As he sits to rest, he falls asleep. After about an hour or so, he wakes up and is angry with himself for having fallen asleep. But, he was so tired, he knew his body needed that rest. Now, more determined than ever to get to his destination, he takes to the road once again.

After about eight more miles of walking, he arrives in another town and wants to seek out a hot meal again. He spots a roadside kitchen where a man and his wife have food prepared for passersby who, like him, are on the road to wherever they are going. Quite a few people found places near the stand to rest and eat. This is perfect! The stand is by the road and there is plenty of shade under a huge awning, and he can keep an eye on his donkey. Not that anyone is about to take Chaver, but Bo doesn't trust anyone at this point and realizes that anything can happen. He isn't paranoid, it's just that he needs to stay vigilant at all times.

It is now about four o'clock and he's made fair progress. If he can just go another three or four miles before calling it a day, he would only have another fifteen or so miles to go the next day. He finishes his meal and after feeding and watering Chaver, continues on his way. He walks until the sun begins to set at about six o'clock. He then begins to look for a place to spend the night. There is nothing in sight except a farm where a family lives.

He thinks to himself:
"I'll ask if it would be alright to sleep in their barn for the night, and tell them that I've been walking a long time and am very tired."

He approaches the house and is met by the landowner, an elderly man. He makes his request, and after thinking about it a moment, the old man agrees. He tells Bo where to put his donkey so he can get a drink and feed on the straw. He then leads him to the barn. The day has lost its light now. The farmer gives Bo an oil lamp so that he can see what he's doing as he deals with his baggage that he unloaded from Chaver. They bid each other "good night," and the farmer returns to the house.

Bo sits a while and thinks about home; his family and friends and all the familiar surroundings. After an hour or so, he feels very tired and figures it's time to bed down.

He thinks to himself:
"It will be a good night. Thank you Lord for this provision. I am grateful. Praise be to You Lord!"

Once again, he hides his money in the barn for the night, wraps it in a cloth away from where he's going to sleep. He puts it in a corner under some straw. He then makes himself a nice bed out of the clean straw in the barn – the best bed so far of his journey. As he lay there, he is calm and not anxious about anyone coming in to rob him in the night. The old man must have looked upon him as a son and taken pity. Again, we see the heart of a father in action. He had come upon the perfect place to stay. This night will be the best sleep he's had since leaving home.

While he lay there before drifting off to sleep, his mind goes back home again. He sees his father's face with tears in his eyes as he left and this brings tears to his own eyes. His brother's face flashes in his mind and he feels bad about the look his brother gave him as he left – a look of disapproval and sadness. This cuts him to the heart for he looked up to Amon. It was Amon who taught him to shear sheep and how to use the walking stick as a weapon. He taught him certain strikes that would disable opponents; as was evident when he intervened in that incident earlier. Even as young boys, it was Amon who would be there to protect him when bullies threatened him. And now, he left everyone to go after his own dreams. The bad feelings last for a good while, but then, he tells himself that he needs to shake off such feelings, for he was going to start a brand new life. He didn't want personal feelings to interfere with that.

Day Five – The Last Day – And the Sabbath

As usual, Bo is up with the sun shining and the roosters crowing. He isn't far from his final destination, but today at sunset, the Sabbath will begin, and he does not want to sin against it. He makes sure he goes to a well to wash his hands and face. A bit later on the road, he finds a stream where he is able do a full body immersion to get completely clean. But, the washing of hands is part of the Jewish daily ritual he was made to observe as a child and still does to this day. He wants to continue to observe his people's ways and thus, respect God, by doing what is known as the morning hand washing (Netilat yadayim shacharit – raising the hands in the morning). This is one way of staying connected to his roots and heritage. This would always be a part of him, so he thinks! It's interesting how quickly things can change.

He not only sees that he is in a foreign land, but he also feels it. Perhaps it's the fact that he is now in a land where the god that rules the hearts of the people there is not the God of his people – the God he knows as Yahweh – the true and living God, maker of heaven and earth. There is a different spirit dwelling there. This indeed will be more than just an experience of being among foreigners. He will need to be careful not to let himself forsake the ways of his people.

He makes his way nearer and nearer toward Beirut and can see outlying towns and villages near the great metropolis as he gets closer. He is now about eight miles from his final destination. He pushes harder now than he had done on all the other days. He'd had an early start and needed to be in Beirut before sunset. He prays that God will make this last part of his journey safe and fast. He walks at a steady pace with a rhythm that seems almost magical. Maybe it's the eagerness in his heart to finally see a city he'd only heard about and all the marvelous things he expects to see. This spurs him on to get there as quickly as he can.

He comes by a stream and is reminded that he needs to wash completely. It's as good a place to do this and give his beast a drink, food and rest. He goes to a secluded place, away from the road, and takes care of his donkey, watering and feeding him. Once the donkey has his fill, he ties him to a small tree so that he can be shaded as he rests. He then goes to the stream where it cuts into the bank a bit, for privacy. As he undresses, he realizes that the money strapped to him needs to be secure.

In the back of his mind, father's words ring again:
"Trust no one! Only God!"

He looks to make sure no one is around, places the bag behind a log and covers it with dead leaves. He finished disrobing and goes into the water to bathe quickly. He washes as fast as he can and exits the water, dries off, gets dressed and takes time to eat, have a drink and rest a while before striking out again. He unties Chaver and takes time to thank God for the good day so far. Although Bo has all these wild ideas as to what he might do once he reaches his destination. He has a heart for God and the good sense of not abandoning the teachings of his mother and father. He knows that at any given moment, things can change and that he would need to rely on the God of heaven and earth to see him through. This is part of the reality of the people of Israel, his people. He knows his people's history well and all that God has done for them in the past. He holds these things dear in his heart.

As he gets closer and closer, he can see the city of Beirut in the distance much clearer. His heart leaps and a huge smile comes across his face. He marvels at how large the city is compared to Nazareth. It is indeed magnificent, even from a distance. Compared to Nazareth, it is massive! His pace is now even faster than ever. He can't wait to get there. All sorts of thoughts come into his mind as he walks. He thinks about what sort of things he will do, where he will go and the people he will meet. He wants to mingle with businessmen in this big city so that he can perhaps find out how or where one can invest money in order to make even more, through good investments.

Finally - Beirut: Sights and Sounds

As he makes his way to the outskirts of Beirut, he can hear the hustle and bustle of the hoard of people and animals that clutter the outside of the city. He notices that there is a distinct smell in the air from the mixture of all there is; the open markets, the open pits where people are cooking food, the spices, the flowers and incenses that burn here and there. All of it hits Bo's senses; his eyes, ears, and nose. His heart is racing! He can't wait to get settled in.

He makes his way through the gates of the city and is questioned by guards. They want to know where he is going. He tells them that he just arrived and would like find a place to stay. They tell him that he must find a stable for his animal in the city proper. He assures them that he will place Chaver in a stable; and that he plans on settling in Beirut permanently.

One of the guards tells Bo where he can find an inn that can accommodate both him and the donkey. He is told the buyers and sellers can only do business in designated market areas with their stands. And, parking their beasts of burden that carry merchandise in or out of the area, have specific areas away from residential areas. He tells Bo that only the locals are allowed to have their animals at or near their homes, and that they have to clean up the streets when their animals leave their droppings.

He saw several stables outside the gates as he made his way in. Seeing that there aren't many beasts of burden inside the city limits, he surmises that some of the residents must place their animals there and retrieved them there if they need to travel. That makes good sense to him.

He takes in all of the commerce going on as he makes his way deeper into the city. He wants to place Chaver in a stable, find a room in an inn, freshen up, eat and get ready before nightfall. The Sabbath will start at sunset. He goes a few blocks, and finds the inn. He ties off his donkey in back of the inn where there is a place for such animals, and walks in the back door, finds the innkeeper and asks about obtaining a room. He is asked how long he would need the room.

Bo says:
"For now, I will need one for at least a week until I find a permanent place. I plan on settling here for a good while and go into business."

The innkeeper Amed, replies:
"It will cost you ten assirions in advance young man. My maid Sabah will show you where it is. As for looking for a permanent place, I know where you can find one. My cousin Fadil has a place ready to rent or to buy, whichever you'd like. We will talk tomorrow. Please, Sabah, show the young man to his room!"

BO SETTLES IN HIS ROOM

He pays Amed, and Sabah shows him to his room. As he enters, it looks fine, with plenty of room for one person. He gets his belongings from his donkey with Sabah's help and brings them in. He gives her one prutah for assisting him. He asks Sabah if it would be okay with her boss if he asked her to tend to his donkey while he stays at the inn, that he would pay her two prutahs a day.

Sabah answers:
"Yes! This way I can make some extra money and it doesn't take very much time to feed one animal. I can do that quickly before I am due to work in the inn. And, at the end of the day, I will tend to him again so that he is set for the night."

The sun will soon set. Bo thanks Sabah and says that he must prepare for prayer, that he will see her in the morning to pay her for her services.

He begins to settle in the room which consists of a bed, a table, two chairs along with a sort of dry sink with a large clay bowl, a good size pitcher of water and a hand towel. Also in the room, there is a chamber pot for obvious reasons. He is in town and this part of personal needs has to be done just so—all the waste is taken care of in an appropriate manner. The maids take care of disposing such refuse.

He goes to the basin of water and begins the ritual washing in preparation for the start of the Sabbath. He washes and changes into clean clothes, and then, just before the sun goes down, he lights the two ritual candles, prepares the two small loaves of challah representing a dual portion of manna, and a small cup of wine.

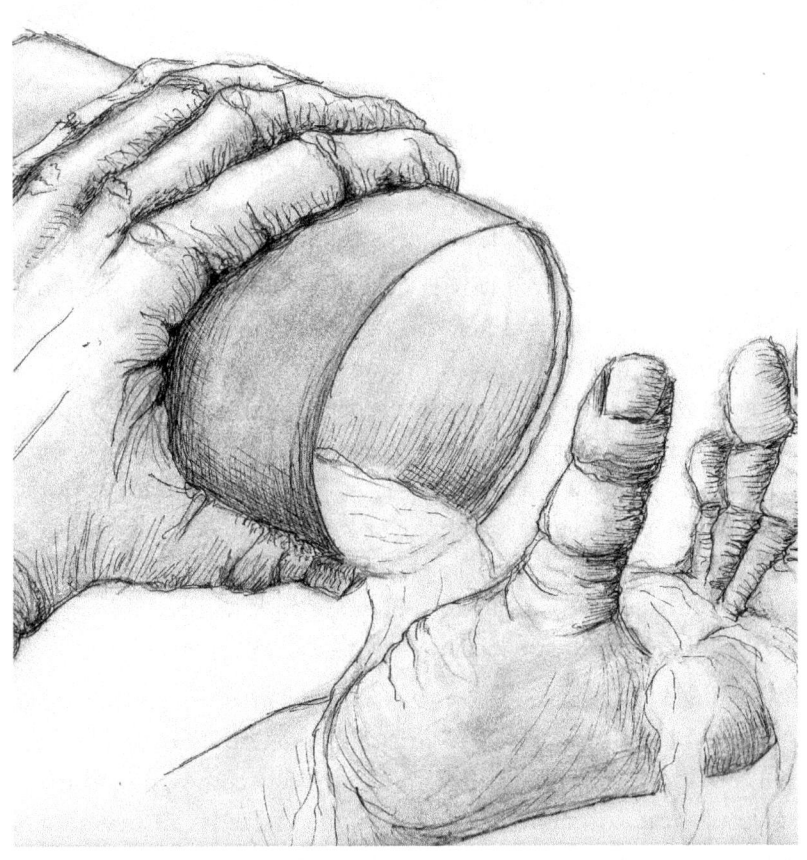

He covers his eyes so as not to see the candles before reciting the blessing from the scroll that he brought along in the small sack. He begins the prayer as follows…

(It must be noted that the prayer is actually much longer. But, here is its beginning.)

Blessed are you, Lord, our God, sovereign of the universe.
Barukh atah Adonai, Eloheinu, melekh ha-olam

Who has sanctified us with His commandments and commanded us
asher kidishanu b'mitz'votav v'tzivanu

to light the lights of Shabbat. (Amen)
had'lik neir shel Shabbat. (Amein)

After having finished the prayer ritual, he thinks of going out for a short walk near the inn, just to see what is around this immediate area. Before he leaves, he wants to make sure the bulk of his money is safe. He needs to find a very safe place for it and not carry it with him everywhere he goes. It is a bit cumbersome. He wonders where can he put it in the room where it will be safe? He lies down on the bed to rest a bit before taking his walk. He closes his eyes and thinks about where to hide the money. As he opens his eyes and looks up at the corner of the room where the ceiling and wall meet, he notices a good size gap between the rafter and the roof covering. He steps up on a stool and reaches in to see how deep the gap is. It's just big and deep enough to store his money. He uses some hay he got from the stable and shoves it in to make it look like a poor effort to seal the gap. He takes a few shekels, staters, and assirions to spend. He feels comfortable with the way the money is hidden and prays that God will protect it.

Now, comfortable that his money is safe, he goes out and stays within the "Sabbath's day walk," (3/5th of a mile) so as to not dishonor the Lord. The dark of night has not completely come yet, and there is enough light left to allow him to see some of the locals in action. He takes a look around all sides of the inn. On one of the sides, he can see a couple of men arguing in the distance. As he looks to his left, he sees and hears one of those "painted ladies" sweet-talking a middle-aged man. Across the street from the inn, he sees a very poorly dressed beggar trying to get money from passers-by. He can hear the cry of babies from several houses. He can also hear a dad yell to his kids to get in the house because it's getting dark. He notices a number of city guards walking around, warning people about the curfew and one of them telling a donkey owner to pick up the mess his animal has just made.

Bo gets very angry when he hears a woman screaming and sees a drunken man beating her with repeated slaps to the face and head. He is furious! He wants to intercede, but realizes that he might be meddling in something he should not. Instead, he gets the attention of one of the guards who then approaches the couple and tells the man to stop, and warns him to treat his woman right, or be put in jail! The man ceases his battering, apologizes to the guard and his woman; puts his arm around her and walks off. This tells Bo that there is at least some order here with the guards patrolling the streets. He's had enough for the night. It is nearly nine o'clock. He makes his way to his room, washes, prays, and goes to bed.

LONG TERM LODGING AND A BUSINESS

The next day, he goes to speak to the innkeeper, Amed. As soon as he walks in, Amed motions him over and tells him again about his cousin Fadil who has a small house for rent or sale – depending on the client's wishes. Amed tells him that it would be three denarius a month to rent it. Bo says he'd like to see the place. Amed tells him that he'd take him there himself at noon. He also asks about a sign he saw outside one of the city gates about a shearing, spooling and blanket-making plant that is looking for someone who would like to buy part of the business. Amed tells him that he knows the owner and that the man is getting a bit too old to manage it by himself anymore and is looking for a partner. He says that the business does well, that it needs a younger man's touch for the operation. He asks the innkeeper if he knows how much it would cost to buy into the business? Amed tells him, around three hundred fifty denarius. He says that he'd be very interested in speaking to the owner.

With that, Amed says:

"I think we're going to be very good friends. The owner Jamal is my wife's uncle. I will take you there tomorrow to make the deal and I'll take you this afternoon to see my cousin Fadil's house that's for rent....or sale, whichever you'd like."

GOING TO MARKET

It's early morning. Bo leaves the inn and figures he'd take a walk through some of the streets before meeting up with Amed at noon. He inquires where the nearest street market is from a young man. The young man tells him there is one three blocks east of the inn where he's staying. He makes his way there and as he nears the market place, a young lady taps him on the back and asks if he is new in the city.

He replies,
"Yes."

She asks if he needs someone to assist him in getting around or to find places where he'd like to go. He simply says that he is going to the market and that he is fine for now. He thanks her for offering to help, and moves along.

He makes his way to the market, and finds it very easily. He can see people walking from there carrying bought goods in baskets. He notes how many are going to and from the market. He thinks to himself that this is a very busy city and that his chances of doing well, is going to be good!

As he walks into the market itself, he observes all the different and new things for sale from the venders: cloth materials of all kinds, clothing, spices, and foods of all sorts. He notices the great variety in looks, speech and clothing styles. This is somewhat amazing to him.

He goes through the market and picks up some fruit, bread and a skin of wine and another for water, since he'd given the latter away to the poor family. The wine skin he has is getting old. He wants to treat himself to something new from the city where he will live. He spends a couple of hours there, then, remembers he needs to be back at the inn to go with Amed to check out the house for sale or rent.

He quickly heads back toward the inn and as he is doing that, he looks down one of the side streets and sees another part of the city. From his vantage point, he can see several inns with a lot of "women of the street" and many men of all ages walking into cottage-type dwellings with their arm around the ladies. He isn't naïve. He knows exactly what is going on. This is the proverbial "red light district," with inns/bars, drinking, women, and plenty of wild and carefree times.

He arrives at the inn, goes to his room, washes his hands and face then goes to meet up with Amed who is waiting for him to take him to his cousin's house. Bo wants to have something to eat and drink before leaving. He does so, and after about an hour, they leave the inn and arrive at Fadil's house mid-afternoon. Amed introduces Bo to Fadil, who takes him a few doors down to show him the place. It is big enough, with three rooms, a main living room with a bed, a kitchen/dining room combination, and a room for bathing. He likes that! It will do fine. He tells him that he likes it, and asks, how much it would cost to buy it, and when he can he move in? Fadil tells him, 100 denarius, and that he can move in right away.

Bo thinks for a moment ...

"Let's see 350 denarius for the business, if that deal goes through, and another 100 for the house. That leaves me with nearly 550 denarius to live on until receiving money from the business. With the profits, I will be able to regain what I've put into the business and come out ahead in the end."

Bo says:

"I'll buy it!"

He tells Fadil he will come by in the morning with the money and his belongings. Fadil is very happy and thanks him for being so prompt in his decision.

Bo feels good about the deal he's made. He takes time to pause on his way back to the inn and prays to God:

"Lord, I place the house You have given me today, in your hands, and ask that You bless it. May You bless my coming in and my going out. Also, the business I will look at tomorrow, please give me wisdom with the negotiations. As I begin this new part of my life, I pray that in doing this, I will honor my father's wishes to do well with the money he gave me and that this dwelling will be a good place – Amen!"

After returning to his room in the inn, he begins to gather his belongings and makes ready for the next day. He summons Sabah the maid, and asks if she'd be willing to take care of his new house after her work is done in the inn. She is only sixteen years old, with no other responsibilities, only the inn. Bo tells her that he will need her to bring him water every day from the well a short distance from the house, go to the market for food, and take care of his donkey Chaver; to feed and give him water. She agrees. He will pay her one denarius a week for her work. Sabah is very pleased. The extra money will help her family. Her widowed mother has three other little ones to care for besides her. He tells her to meet him mid-morning so he can show her where his house is located. She tells him she will be prompt.

THE MOVE INTO THE NEW HOUSE

Morning comes. Bo is up at the break of day, washes, gets dressed and eats. He then goes out to the stable to bring Chaver to the inn and loads his belongings. As he is doing that, Sabah shows up as she said she would. In being prompt, he knows he has chosen well in asking her to be his maid. She showed good character. Bo tells her to wait outside. He goes in to retrieve the money he has hidden. They leave and head for his new place, about a half mile walk from the inn.

They get to Fadil's house mid-morning. Bo pays him the money. Fadil signs the deed and gives it to Bo. He shows Sabah where the house is and tells her that he expects her to take care of the tasks he had spoken to her about, every day. Sabah leaves and Bo goes into his small sack to get a mezuzah to place on his doorpost.

He nails it there and recites the prayer:

"Baruch atta Adonai Eloheinu malech ha'olam, asher kideshanu be-mitzvotav vetzivanu likboa' mesuzah."

> *(Blessed are You, Lord our Lord, King of the universe, who sanctified us with His mitzvoth, (commandment) and commanded us to affix a mezuzah)*

With that done, he feels very good. This is now his place, his home, and he has honored God by placing the mezuzah as is custom among his people. Before he enters, he touches the mezuzah, brings his hand back to his lips and kisses it. In a way, he has christened his new abode.

THE BUSINESS

The following day, Bo goes back to the inn to meet Aman so that he can take him to see his wife's uncle to talk about buying in his cotton processing, sheep shearing and blanket-making business. He gets there early in the morning and Aman is ready to escort him to the factory.

As they enter the plant, he notices that Jamal is somewhat elderly, a bit hunched over and seems to have difficulty walking. The three talk about the business together and Jamal shows Bo around and introduces him to the people who already work there.

The building is fairly large and the coral can hold at least 250 sheep. He has contraptions to turn raw wool and cotton into spools of yarn and thread which are used to make blankets, and wearing apparels. He also sells some of the spools to another man nearby who has everything set up to make material for clothing, linen articles, curtains, tablecloths, scarves, head wear, blankets and so on. Bo thinks this will be a good thing! He is very pleased that he came upon this deal.

After a lot of talking over a bit of food and wine to settle all the business details of how the profits will be shared, Bo feels comfortable going forward and agrees on the price of three hundred and fifty denarius and becomes Jamal's partner. He says he will return the next morning to pay him. Jamal says he will have the contract ready for both to sign. They shake hands, and with the deal now done, Amed and Bo leave and head back to the inn.

NEW ENCOUNTERS

The next day arrives, and Bo is eager to get started with his new business. First, he needs to go and settle the money matter with Jamal. He takes the amount needed from the inheritance money he has hidden in his house. He makes his way to Jamal's house and pays him what he owes. Jamal and Bo sign two contracts, one for each of them to keep. After taking care of all legal matters, Bo goes to have a meeting with the plant's employees.

He meets Kasib, who manages the business, makes contact with cotton farmers and sheep herders who bring in their sheep for shearing, and paying them. He too, does some of the shearing and sets up the spool-making machines. Then, there is Abdul the foreman. He and two other younger men take care of most of the shearing and making blankets. Also in the plant, there are two young women who help with all of the tasks and are in charge of storing the finished products. They also prepare noonday meals for the men and themselves. They are, Jamila and Ella. Both are in their early twenties and attractive. They will become intimate companions with Bo as time goes on. Jamila and Ella are delighted to meet Bo, and find him very handsome. From day one, both of the ladies have ideas about the new business partner.

After all the wool and cotton is processed into spools, Abdul and the young men take some of the surplus material to be sold to one of the weaving plants. The money paid for the goods is taken back to the two partners and distributed in a business-like manner. Each partner gets his share. The employees are paid and some is put aside to pay business costs. Things go very well for the first few months. Bo is well-pleased with his investment. There is a steady flow of herds coming in to be sheared and the whole process continues without problems.

NEW FRIENDS & LIFESTYLE

He now has a whole new life going, complete with a new home, a business venture and new acquaintances. As time goes on, His workers become his new friends. Since he is single and has no one to cook for him, they invite him to their homes for dinners and special events. It comes to pass that Ella is the first to take a special interest in Bo, and he is attracted to her as well. We cannot forget Jamila, the other worker, however. She too is pretty, and has amorous ideas concerning him. Not only are these two lovely young ladies vying for his affections, but also two maids from Abdul's inn, Sophia and Mia, have expressed an interest in the newcomer to the city. (The young maid Sabah is not part of that mix.)

As the days go by, Ella invites Bo to dinner at her house. She divorced the year before and had several suitors, but no one special. He accepts her invitation and goes to her house. They eat and then sit to talk a while. As she serves him a drink of wine and hands it to him, she touches his face in a loving way, and Bo's life takes a turn at that point. They share an intimate evening. He leaves late in the evening and returns to his house.

As he is walking, he thinks to himself:
"This is great! I like being my own man. I don't have to explain myself to anyone for what I do. I'm free to do as I please. That's one of the

reasons I'm here; to live life the way I want to live it. I really enjoyed being with Ella. Something new has awakened in me and I like it!"

The next day at the plant, Bo greets everyone including Ella, who smiles and winks at him secretly.

He gets the message, as if to say,
"Remember last night?"

Bo smiles back at her then goes ahead and begins to take care of the work at hand.

Ella and Jamila prepare the noon day food for the crew and serves them when it is ready. Ella is quick to serve Bo first, before Jamila is able to get the chance. She secretly squeezes his arm after serving him. But, Jamila catches the gesture out of the corner of her eye. Woman's intuition tells Jamila that something is up. When it comes time to clean up the table, Jamila asks Ella what is going on. Having worked together for a long time, they know each other well and are very good friends. Ella tells her what had happened and that she is very fond of Bo, but that they are not committed. With that bit of information, Jamila tells Ella that she'd like to invite him to her house. Ella is a bit slighted but knows that Bo doesn't belong to anyone, at least not yet. She finds Bo alone and asks if he would come over after work to help her fix a broken chair she has at home, and that she would feed him as well. He tells her that he would be very happy to do it.

AT JAMILA'S HOUSE

After the work day is done, Jamila waits till all the others are gone and leads Bo to her house. She shows him the chair to be fixed. He begins fixing it right away. As he is fixing the chair, he needs another pair of hands to hold the two parts in place while he ties the cord to hold them together. He asks Jamila to help. She holds the pieces while Bo wraps and ties the cord very tight to secure the loose parts. As he is finishing, Jamila's face is close to his and she kisses his cheek. He reacts by drawing her to him, and kisses her. He finds himself again in a similar situation as the one he had experienced the night before. They too spend an evening together. After he leaves Jamila's house, he thinks about his last two nights.

He thinks:

"Wow Bo, you're a lucky man! Two evenings in a row with two lovely women."

He feels very alive! These new events have brought excitement in his life. At long last, he is able to cut himself loose from all the moral restraints he experienced under the watchful eyes of his father, brother and sisters, In Nazareth, everyone knew him and expected proper conduct from him. But now, he is on his own and is taking full advantage of it.

He goes home, bathes, and goes to bed. Before falling asleep, all that had happened runs through his head. Part of him is excited and part of him is troubled a bit. He is caught between two worlds—that of his people with reverence towards God's commandments and the wild and carefree life of his new surroundings in Beirut.

Being his father's son, his father's words hit him again:

"Be very careful of the women you encounter?"

He tosses that around in his mind for a while, but the excitement of his experiences win over.

He reasons:

"I'm my own man now and I want to experience this kind of life. It feels good! It feels right! I'm enjoying my life now. I feel I have purpose, not like being on the farm with nothing exciting to look forward to!"

He now has a whole new mind-set and lifestyle - that of a carefree, fun-loving, drinking, woman-chasing young fool! This is not good!

The Next Day - Confronting the Issue at Hand

Bo rises the next day and goes to work. As he enters the plant, he sees both Ella and Jamila. Jamila is smiling but Ella has the look of a woman scorned! Right away, he knows that this is not going to be a good thing. Jamila evidently told Ella about her time with Bo. The day goes on with the men doing their tasks and the women doing theirs. The women keep their distance from each other. When it comes time to break for the mid-day meal, it is Jamila this time who serves Bo. Ella stays away and is very quiet.

At the end of the work day, he asks Ella privately to stay behind so he can talk to her. She does so and meets with him. He tells her that he is sorry for what he had done. He tells her that it just happened, that he should have resisted Jamila's approach, but that something in him just couldn't. She understands, but is still angry with him. She asks him who he wants; her or Jamila? He thinks for a moment and says that both of them are very special but that he cannot not make a decision. Ella gets angry and tells him that he needs to come to a decision one way or another. As she is leaving, she tells him that she cares for him very much and that she would be a good woman for him. She leaves it at that, knowing that in the matters of the heart, no one can force love, that it has to come naturally.

Bo watches her leave and thinks to himself that he'll need to come up with some kind of solution for the awkward situation he finds himself in. He likes both, Ella and Jamila equally. He is unable to completely surrender his heart to either one. He doesn't want to lose them. He'd like to court them both, but realizes that this will get a bit complicated. He shakes off the concern for the moment and leaves the plant.

NEW LADIES IN BO'S LIFE

As He makes his way home, he stops at Amed's inn to eat something and have a little wine to take his mind off the chat he had with Ella. His servant at the inn is Sophia. She is very friendly and pretty. As she waits on him, she becomes a bit flirtatious and gives gentle touches to his back as she walks by his table to go to another. Also in the inn is Mia, another servant. Mia is not as pretty as Sophia but still good-looking to Bo. To him, she is more genuine and down to earth. He finishes eating and asks for another drink of wine. He lingers there talking to Amed and a few of the other men.

One of the men says to Bo:
"I think Sophia would like a new husband."

Bo asks what he meant, and the man tells him that she keeps looking his way. He tells him that she is indeed very nice but that he would prefer Mia if he were looking for a wife. He does not see her, but Mia is standing only a couple of paces behind him and hears everything. That puts a smile on her face and ideas in her head.

It is getting late, and he needs to go home and sleep. As he gets up from his table, he is a bit tipsy and nearly falls to the floor.

Amed tells Sophia:
"It's almost closing time. Why don't you walk Bo home to make sure our young friend makes it there safely?"

He would ask one of the men, but they are in pretty much the same shape Bo is in. To steady him, Sophia puts her arm around his waist and puts his arm over her shoulder and holds his hand. Once they get inside the house, Bo is uninhibited enough to say to Sophia that she is very beautiful, and kisses her. His move is more than welcome to Sophia. He falls into temptation again. She stays with him for the next four hours to help him sober up and take care of him. Afterwards, she leaves and he falls asleep. Waking in the morning with a light headache and a very sour stomach, he replays the night before in his head. He knows he has done something he probably shouldn't have, but it felt good and right, in his heart.

He makes it to work and puts in a full day. It is not a day without stress. He needs to be cordial to both Jamila and Ella without showing too much affection to either one. Because of his behavior, neither of the ladies can figure out which one he will eventually choose, not knowing that he doesn't intend to make a choice, but just wants to play the field.

Finally, the day is finished. He's glad. It"s Friday, and by sunset, he knows he has to be ready to keep the Sabbath again, but he isn't really looking forward to it.

As he gets ready to leave at about four in the afternoon, the boys say to him:
"Come with us for a quick drink to celebrate the very profitable week we had."

The company has made a good amount of money. Bo figures he's earned a little time to celebrate his good fortune and joins the men.

He thinks to himself:
"I've worked very hard this week and deserve to enjoy the fruit of my labors like any other man."

Off they go to the area Bo had seen a while back when he was going to see Fadil to seal the deal about the house.... the red light district. Once there, he sees things going on between men and women that he's not seen before.

One of the men with him sees the expression on his face and says:
"Are you ready for some fun and excitement?"

Bo replies with a grin:
"I'm not sure if I belong here. This is a very wild place, and there is so much that is very new to me. Besides, I must be home before sunset!"

One of the men taunts him:

"Are you a man or are you a boy? This is what real living is all about. Stay with us! I promise you won't regret it, my friend. We'll have a great time! You only live once!"

Bo tells them he'll have one drink with them and then he'd have to get home. They laugh and bring him into one of the establishments. There, he sees some of the most beautiful ladies he's ever seen, all of them seductively dressed, and with painted faces. They smell so good and are extremely friendly. There are no restraints. Men and women are having their way with one another as if they have no moral codes whatsoever. At first, Bo is somewhat shocked, then as he drinks with the others, he himself, begins to lose his inhibitions. A young lady comes and sits on his lap and kisses him. He kisses her right back! The men laugh and tell Bo that he has found his lady for the evening. She brings him another drink and continues to entice him. After a few more drinks, he is no longer in control. She sweet-talks him into going for a walk. That walk takes him to her place. Once there, he cannot resist her charms and falls yet another time.

Realizing the sun has long set, Bo has missed observing the Sabbath. He feels bad, but not that bad. He lingers with the woman for a while longer before leaving. He leaves the harlot's house and makes his way home. The effects of the drinks have diminished some and he is able to think somewhat more clearly. He thinks about all he had done lately. This makes him feel good. He likes the idea of being his own man, and doing what he wants to do.

That's the good side of how he feels. Then he realizes that his money pouch is missing. He had around four minas ($140) when he entered the inn with the boys. The harlot had taken it. He can't remember exactly where she lives or even what she looks like. He only saw her in dimly lit quarters. He chalks it up as his loss for being so stupid as to trust a harlot.

Now in his house, he blames God and gets angry at Him, for not protecting him against bad company and the thieving harlot. He is changing. He has enjoyed several forbidden things: the women he's been with so far, and the daily drinking with the men at Amed's inn. He goes to bed and while falling asleep, he relives those new good times he's had. This change in his behavior is not good.

SATURDAY – THE SABBATH DAY

He wakes up and reflects on the night before. He remembers having a good time, and is looking forward to doing some of the same tonight. He says a few prayers in keeping with the Sabbath, but his heart is not in it. His mind is now on how much fun he can have. It's like he is addicted to the new experiences he's been having lately. He wants more and more of the same. He realizes that he has weaknesses; women and wine. He tells himself that he needs to be careful with the ladies he has met so far, and with his drinking.

Another thought comes to mind:
"This is easier said than done."

Since it is still the Sabbath, (until sunset) he devotes his day to relaxing. After a while, he wants to go into the city. He doesn't hold to the "Sabbath day's walk" (three fifths of a mile - round trip) He walks to Amed's inn that is a half mile away to eat and to down a few cups of wine. Sophia is working and she asks Bo if they can get together later. He doesn't hesitate. He says, "Yes." They come together once more and this time, Bo becomes like one of the free-spirited young men of the city. He takes full advantage of Sophia's friendship and all that she has to offer.

This arrangement goes on for quite a while. He even gets to spend time with Mia, but not as often as he does with Sophia. When he is with Sophia, he tells her not to say anything to Mia, and when he is with Mia, he tells Mia not to say anything to Sophia The two ladies do not share their amorous experiences with each other the way Jamila and Ella did. Bo relishes playing the field with the ladies, but is also very focused on the business. He takes time to sup with his partner Fadil and his wife. They talk business mostly and he enjoys being with them.

Fadil treats him like a son. This makes him feel like he has some kind of "family" connection. "

Bo's Beating

One night, Bo goes by that night-life street again with the thought of maybe seeing the harlot who had stolen his money. By chance, there she is! He does remember her. He approaches her and demands she give him his money. Nearby is the girl's boyfriend and confronts him, telling him that he'd better leave. Bo tells him that she had stolen from him and that he just wanted his money back. All of a sudden, someone strikes him on the head with a club. He is knocked out and robbed again! Whatever he has on him is now gone, about $100. After waking up behind an inn, he struggles to his feet and thinks that he should leave that area and never return.

He makes it home with a wicked headache. He puts a wet, cool cloth on his head, lies down and falls asleep. He wakes up the next day still having the headache, but he has to get to work. He goes there and tells the boys what had happened and that he'd never go out with them again. He tells them that they should not have urged him to drink and carouse. From that time on, the men distance themselves from Bo. He pretty much becomes "just the boss" and they, the hired hands. They've seen the change in him, and know this about him - that he has two weakness; women and the wine.

Drinking, Loose Talk, and Women

Bo continues having affairs with Ella, Jamila, Sophia and Mia. He also visits another part of the city where the night life is wild and crazy. He befriends a whole new crowd of people which includes many other ladies, and spends time with them the way he'd been doing with the others. Besides the carousing and drinking, Bo develops a taste for bad jokes and foul language with regards to comments he makes toward some of the women and men around him. This new change in him is a very bad thing. It can only get worse for him. He is now heading in a direction he should not be. His father's counsel is fading fast. He has abandoned a righteous life for one that is completely contrary to the way he was raised. He is now, "a man of the world."

All this mixing it up with harlots, bad friends, and drinking, costs Bo money. Little by little, his money is being wasted away on good times, and at the rate he is going, he will soon be broke unless he turns things around. He only has a couple of hundred denarius left from his initial inheritance and the profits from the business. He has gotten used to playing it up big to impress friends and the ladies. He's in the habit over-paying the ladies for their time and has loaned money to a few false friends who have no intention of paying him back. He's been gone from home two and a half years and things aren't looking good for him.

Bo has forsaken his father's words:
"Trust no one! Only God!" He is hooked on worldly things and has forsaken God!"

Famine – Bankruptcy - Employment

A few years have passed, and it looks like a famine is about to hit - and it does! Little by little, the famine takes its toll and, the sheep herds get smaller and smaller. Jamal and Bo have to let Jamila and Ella go as well as the two helpers and the manager. Bo has to go out himself to drum up business. The regular herdsmen have had to slaughter many of their sheep for food. They too, are bad off. With smaller herds, many of the herdsmen find themselves shearing their remaining sheep themselves, which cuts out the need for Bo's and Jamal's services for them.

Soon, with the combination of his carousing and drinking, the lack of work and the famine, the plant closes! He is okay for a while on what little money he has left, but all of it soon runs out. He tries to get work, but it's no use. No one is hiring. As a matter of fact, the unemployment runs high. It is such a large city and there are so many men in the same situation he is in.

DESTITUTE

It gets to the point where all that he has left are the clothes on his back, his blanket, his house and the bag containing the religious items for the Sabbath. The small house is the only equity he has. He's even sold his donkey Chaver for a fraction of what he was worth. With that money, he is able to hold on for a few days, but that too runs out. Now what!? He is getting more and more desperate. He finally sells his house back to Fadil, expecting at least, the same amount he had paid (a hundred denarius), but Fadil tells him that he too is not doing well financially. Fadil can only give him forty denarius - only a little less than half of what he had paid him. He takes it. There is nothing else he can do. He can at least stretch that amount to cover bare expenses for a couple of months, maybe more.

From Fadil's house, Bo goes to Amed's inn to see if he can rent the same room he had had when they first met. Amed still has it available. Feeling sorry for him, he charges him one denarius a week instead of the two he would normally charge. After a few weeks, Bo finds himself destitute. He foolishly spent some of what he had left on drinks and ladies – again! He is now completely out of money and no job. He goes to a few of the people (friends) to whom he had loaned money to see if they could help him out. None of them is able to help. He is tapped out with no prospect of being helped by anyone. All his "so-called-friends" have abandoned him!

With no money and no friends, he makes his way to Jamila's house to see if she can take him in. She rebuffs him coldly! The same thing happens when he goes to Ella's house and to Sophia at the inn. He doesn't dare go to poor Sabah's house (his former maid) for he knows that she, her mother, and siblings also must be in bad shape financially due to the famine. What to do?

He finds himself out on the streets begging like many other destitute individuals. He eats scraps of food he finds tossed out behind some of the inns. On a few rare occasions, some good-hearted people actually let him come into their house so he can be fed. But, he can't keep coming back to the same generous people. He starts looking very haggard and dirty. His clothes smell and are looking very shabby, and his sandals have worn out. He is bare foot! He is now an official vagabond; homeless, and jobless. He is a prime example of intense poverty.

He walks off to place of solitude to be alone, sits down under a tree, and starts thinking about what he can do. He needs a job, food to eat, and shelter. He is as low as he has ever seen anyone be. He is so very miserable that he wants to die.

As he sits to ponder his grave situation; his head is bowed down, his entire being defeated, and his soul in torment. Finally, he looks up at heaven and prays as fervently and as desperately as he has ever done.

He says:

"Father, Lord of the universe. I am so sorry for all the wrong I've done! I have sinned against You and against heaven… please forgive me!!! I am now at the very end of hope to stay alive. I implore you Lord to provide me with those things I need so I can go on living. I will change my ways and come back to you as a son of Abraham, Isaac and Jacob."

DESPERATION / A JOB

It is well known that when men get desperate, they can do desperate things.

Bo thinks to himself,

"I will work for anyone for no pay, just sustenance and lodging.

He goes to various businesses in hope of getting food and shelter in exchange for work. No one wants to agree to those terms and everyone turns him away. His desperation gets worse and worse until he comes upon a man who is bringing pigs to the slaughter house at the edge of the city. The man heard that Bo is looking for work and tells him to follow him home and can work for him for lodging. As for food, the man makes no provisions, only the husks that he feeds the swine.

It must be noted that in Leviticus 11:7-8 it states...

"And the swine, though he divide the hoof, and be cloven footed, yet he cheweth not the cud; he is unclean to you. Of their flesh shall ye not eat, and their carcases shall ye not touch; they are unclean to you." (KJV)

He realizes that as a Jew, it is totally disgraceful allowing himself to do this, but he is desperate. He is repulsed by having to deal with the pigs. He does what is asked of him. He is sent to feed the pigs, and as he stands in the midst of them, ankle deep in the muck and mire, the filth and the awful stench, he reasons that he should have never stooped so low as to feed swine. The pigs are eating, but he is starving, and no one has compassion on him.

He thinks to himself:

"Here I am starving while the swine have food and in my father's house, the servants have plenty, and even some to spare while I stand here starving. I need to go back if I am to save myself and live. I will tell my father that I have sinned against heaven and him and that I am no longer worthy to be called a son. I will beg him to take me back as a hired servant."

HOPE

After this little talk to himself, Bo drops the bushel of corn husks, takes a few for the road and heads towards home. He knows this will be a long and very difficult journey back. He has no money whatsoever, no food, no change of clothes, no blanket to cover him at night and no sandals to make the rough road bearable as he walks. He doesn't even have his trusty walking stick for protection or to lean on. He is a man stripped completely naked of all his possessions and pride. He had never known that kind of existence. He stands as a man now twenty-four years old with all dignity and pride stripped from him.

He finds the road that leads back home and starts walking. The hundred plus miles might kill him, but the only hope he has in the world is getting back home to the care of his father.

The first day's walk ends, and surprisingly, Bo has done a little better than ten miles. He is completely exhausted and hungry. He ate some of the corn husks he took along with him, but it wasn't enough. He feels weak, lacking the strength to go any further. He finds a shelter with some hay and an old, smelly horse blanket and nestles in for the night. He doesn't even think about anyone robbing him like it had happened on the way to Beirut. He has nothing. What can anyone take from him?

THE SECOND DAY

The next morning, he wakes at the sound of a rooster crowing. He goes to a farm and begs for food. The lady of the house sees his miserable condition and takes pity on him. He stands before her in filthy clothing and no sandals or coat. She is older and can only think of her own son being in that condition. She tells him to sit on the stoop of the porch and that she will bring him food. As she brings the food and drink, he thanks her repeatedly, and is so touched by her kindness, he weeps.

She pats his back and says:
"Here, put on this coat. You must be so cold. Now, eat and get your strength back. Where are you going, son?"

Bo responds:

"I'm going home to Nazareth to beg my father's forgiveness for the things I've done. I left him to seek adventure and good times in Beirut. Look at me now! I didn't do very well, did I?"

She replies:
"Sometimes in life we make bad choices. But, after we realize the wrong we've done, we need to do our best to make things right. Take it from a mother's heart, son: a true father's love is very strong. Go to him and make things right! I know he will pardon you."

Bo takes in the food and water given to him. The lady goes in the house and leaves him alone for a while. She returns to see how he is doing. He thanks her again for the food and drink, and her words of encouragement.

He finished eating. He asks if he could stay and rest a while.

She says:

"Yes, of course! Take all the time you need before you finish your journey."

He leans back against one of the porch post, closes his eyes and drifts off to sleep. After about an hour, he wakes up and gets himself mentally ready to continue the journey. The kindly lady hands him a sac with enough food for a couple of days and a gourd of water.

She says to him:

"Remember this: you can't take back the wrong you've done, but you can always be forgiven. Believe in your father's love for you! Salam!"

(Peace!)

He thanks her again, turns towards the road and begins walking. With a lot more miles to go, he has a lot of time to think. As he thinks about seeing the house of his youth again, he smiles and is strengthen by that. The downside of his thoughts is of his father and his brother. His half smile turns to a frown and he becomes anxious about having to face his family. In his state of mind for the things he'd done, he can only speculate as to what kind of reception he'll get. He remembers that his father had pleaded with him not to go! He remembers the very disapproving look on his brother Amon's face and the pain his sisters also felt as they kissed him goodbye. He thinks of the servants and how they too might not be very receptive.

Yes, he is going back home, but to what? Will his father actually forgive him, and take him back as a son, or tell him that he is not forgiven, not welcome, and that he should leave his presence? He runs all sorts of scenarios through his mind and is becoming more and more distraught at the negative possibilities. Yet, he hopes!

He remembers what the old lady had told him:

"A true father's love is very strong. Go to him and make things right!"

He keeps that close to his heart, and it gives him hope. He keeps going. He moves as fast as his bare feet will allow on that harsh road. His feet hurt bad and he has a few cuts that hinder his pace. He bares the pain and every step he takes gets him closer to home where he hopes to be accepted—even if it is as a lowly servant. He feels low, and for good reasons. Bo had failed to see the error of his ways in that foreign land. He let himself fall into temptation and temptation bit him, chewed him up, and spit him out into the cesspool he had created for himself.

He thinks:

"Had I never left; what would I have missed? I would have missed the not-so-nice trip to Beirut, the theft of mom's blanket, the theft of my clothes, the money, the kick in the head, more theft of money, the club to the head, the drunken bouts, the whoring and carousing that eventually led to my ruin."

He realizes that even the good times he had had with the women, all of that was momentary - none of it lasted! And as he thinks about what he got in return, it crushes his heart. He knows he's done so much wrong. A quick picture of the candles lit and the prayer scroll for the Sabbath prayers flash through his mind. He feels so guilty. He no longer has them. Someone had taken them. Oh ... and the mezuza he had nailed to the house; he had forgotten to retrieve it when he sold it back to Fadil. What hurts him more than the items now gone is the fact that he had allowed himself to live like a heathen and had turned away from God! He turned away from God to run blindly into the arms of the things of the world that only offered him misery in the end. He may have lost all his worldly possessions, but he still has his reasoning. He sees how foolish he was and is very angry with himself.

He tries to shut out any more disturbing thoughts, but it's no use. His brother Amon's face creeps into his mind, the brother who had taught him so much as they grew up together, and shared so many good times. The look on Amon's face when he left is still fresh in his mind and that shakes him up. He knows he'll have to face him and what will he say to him? This is not a good walk back home, but one that triggers all sorts of unpleasant thoughts of the reunion. He finally realizes that the long walk back, with bare feet, hungry and raggedy, is God's way of giving him time to reflect on all that had happened: from leaving home, his time in Beirut, the good times, his ruin, and now, his long and arduous walk back in pain and agony, physically, emotionally, and psychologically. He still has a long walk ahead and a lot more time to think.

He has to take many breaks as he walks. He is very weak. He is so thankful for the coat, food and water the good lady had given him. It sustains him. But, with all of the emotions that run through his mind, he's a wreck. He is as one who has lost the will to live. He just doesn't have good feelings about facing everyone back home. He feels that there is so much against him that it will be impossible to start anew and be accepted. His anguish is immense.

Again, the old lady's words encourage him:
"A true father's love is very strong. Go to him and make things right."

He keeps repeating that in his mind, over and over again. But still, there are doubts. Despite the good words from the old lady, Bo is unable to forgive himself. He weeps as he keeps running everything through his mind. He is tormented by how he has dishonored his father, his brother, his sisters and most of all, God!

Fifth Day – Crucial Point

It had taken him five days to walk to Beirut when he left home, but now, since he has no shoes, the pace is much, much slower. It comes to a point where he just can't go on any more! He is about twenty miles from home and his body gives out. His feet are a mess, his legs barely able to support him, and his mind full of doubt and anxiety. His entire being gives up! He lays himself down by the side of the road and hopes that death comes. The food and water the lady had given him are gone. He is starving and thirsty. He would need another two days to get there. As he lies there, a man comes down the road with a bull towing a cart. He sees Bo, and goes to him to see if he is alive. He is motionless and semi-conscious.

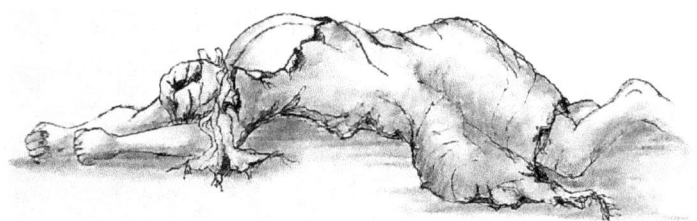

The carter notices how bad Bo looks and takes pity thinking:
"This could be my son! I must help him."

He shakes him to see if he is alive. He moans as he is shaken. Quickly, the man gets a gourd of water and gives him a drink. He carries him to his cart, places him there, and bandages his feet. He figures he's going to one of the small towns in the direction of Nazareth. After a few miles, they arrive in a village.

By then Bo is conscious but still very weak. The lack of food, lack of water and the difficult walk he'd done so far has taken its toll on him. He has lost a lot of weight and his once stocky frame is now skeletal. His countenance is as one who has been totally beaten down. He has no smile. He looks so pitiful. He has difficulty walking. His feet are blistered and have several cuts from rocks in the road. The bandages help, but he isn't ready to take on those extra seventeen miles left to go.

The man tells him he can stay in a room that is attached to his house for a few days if he needs to. He thanks him profusely for the offer but says that he needs to leave in the morning; that he needs to get home. The room is very poorly kept, dirty and dusty with a very uncomfortable cot for him to sleep on. He is given food and water, but very little. The family is poor and can't spare much. As soon as he finishes eating, he lays down. It is sunset. He figures he'd get as much sleep as he could before starting out in the morning. He falls asleep as soon as he lays his head on the cot. He sleeps extremely well, almost as if he had been knocked out. He so needed this sleep and doesn't remember dreaming or waking up throughout the night.

He wakes with the sun. He washes with water from a large bowl that was placed in the room. One of the man's young daughters brings him food. She knocks at the door, he opens it, and she gives him the food without saying a word. She barely looks at him. **Right away he thinks:**

"I must be a sight with these raggedy clothes, gnarled hair, scruffy beard, and bandaged feet."

He eats quickly and musters up strength to get to his feet. He leaves the room and encounters the owner in the yard. He thanks him for his kindness and bids him farewell. The man repeats the offer about staying if he doesn't feel strong enough to leave. Bo tells him he is well enough to go on and that he will go slow to conserve his energy.

On he goes. As he makes his way to finish those last seventeen miles, he starts recognizing some of the hills in the distance. He even comes by a small village where he had been when he was a boy to visit friends of the family for a wedding. He doesn't dare think of stopping in. He would be too ashamed to let them see him in this condition.

He thinks:

"What would they think of me?"

He just keeps walking, each step in pain, but he is determined to make it home before nightfall. He is doing okay until fatigue overcomes him after walking ten miles. He has only seven more miles to go but does not have the strength to continue. He will need a seventh day to finish the journey. But, where will he sleep for the night? He is in the middle of nowhere with nothing but the road before and behind him, and fields all around. He limps to a tree and lies under it. Again, he feels that it would be okay if God took his life right there and then. He has no will to live. He is so beaten up by malnutrition, pain, fatigue and the emotional trauma he's carried all the way home. So close to home and he doesn't have the strength to go on.

He lays there feeling sorry for himself, and at the same time, realizing that the state he is in is his own fault. He falls asleep in a fetal position like a wounded animal waiting for death to end his misery.

He sleeps through the night in that position. He wakes to the sound of bleating sheep a short distance from him. There is a man tending the flock. He limps over to him and asks if he has anything he could spare for him to eat. The man hands Bo a piece of bread wrapped in a cloth and gives him some water as well. He asks Bo where he is going.

Bo tells him:

"Nazareth."

The man tells him that he isn't too far from there.

Bo responds:

"I know. That's where my family is. I've been gone for almost four years and I need to get there today! As you can see, I'm destitute, but my family has plenty. I went off and squandered my inheritance. And now, I have nothing—less than nothing! I've been stripped of all dignity and can no longer be deemed a son of my father because of all the wrong I've done. I would rather be dead, but something is keeping me going."

The man understands his plight but feels that he needs to give Bo a bit of encouragement.

He says:

"Don't say you have nothing! You have your life and life is more precious than anything you can own. You may be defeated now and feel worthless, but you need to remember that God created you in His image! You need to honor that! **Remember, your gift from God is your life, and your gift back to God is what you do with your life."**

It was as though a light went on in Bo's head when the man told him that. He even manages to smile and thanks him for the encouragement and his wise words. He stays with him a while to talk and eat. Bo is refreshed once more and wants to be on his way. He hugs the man and thanks him repeatedly!

As he walks off, he looks up at the heavens and prays:
"Lord, I am not worthy to ask anything, but I humble myself before You to beg Your forgiveness for all that I have done. I implore You to give me the strength to continue and ask that You carry me the rest of the way home."

He is now ready to complete the seven more miles to his father's house. He begins to walk and finds a stick by the road. He picks it up and uses it as a makeshift cane to relieve the pain in his left foot - it is the worst of his two battered feet. Step by step he goes on… one mile, two, three, and eventually, he can see his father's house about a mile and a half ahead as he clears the top of a hill. His heart jumps for joy, and he can't wait to get there! He can't wait to see his father and his sisters, Ruth and Ana. He very much wants to see his brother Amon but is very apprehensive. Again, he remembers the look on his brother's face when he left, that he was extremely disappointed and hurt! Nevertheless, he wants to get home.

He comes closer and closer to his final destination. As he is about a third of a mile away, his father who is sitting on the porch, looks out and sees a figure walking toward the house. He looks hard and squints to get a better look. He sees someone familiar in that frame. Although the figure is limping and staggering a bit, he notes the way he's holding his head, a bit to the side. He's only seen that in his boy, Bo. No one else has that look.

He thinks to himself:
"Can it be him? Can that be my Bo?"

He stands up and approaches the edge of the porch as that unsteady frame comes a bit closer.

He gasps and yells to his daughters in the house:
"Quick, Ruth, Ana, come with me! Hurry! Hurry!"

Amiel knows it's his boy. It is Bo. He yells:
"Bo! My son Bo! Praise God! Praise God!"

The joy of seeing Bo overwhelms him. He runs toward his son as fast as his aging legs can carry him. He can't get there fast enough. He runs, he smiles, he laughs, and finally, there is a slight pause in his step, then he continues running, then, weeps great tears of unspeakable joy!

HE PRAISES GOD!

Some of the servants join in the rush to Bo's side. As Bo sees his father running toward him, he does his best to pick up the pace to go faster and begins to weep sorely because he can see what an effort his father is making to get to him. Finally, Amiel and the girls are only a few paces till they reach him. Amiel slows to a halt, then, walks towards Bo with his arms extended.

"A true father's love is very strong."

Bo has stopped too. He stands there with his head down, his arms at his side, waiting to hear:

"Welcome home Bo."

Amiel just hugs him so tight that he can feel his father's love wash over his entire being. Bo hugs his father right back with all the strength that is left in his emaciated and tired body. Amiel kisses his face and neck repeatedly as he weeps, and thanks God for bringing his son back to him. They just hold onto each other for a good while. As this is going on, Ana and Ruth have wrapped their arms around both of them, connecting hands, and creating one of the most glorious "group hugs" in history. When Amiel finally pulls away but not letting go of one of Bo's hands, he smiles at him, with tears in his eyes.

Bo brakes in and says:

"Father, I have sinned against heaven, and in your sight, and am no longer worthy to be called your son. I'm so sorry ..."

Amiel cuts him short and shushes him as a loving dad would do to a hurting child.

He tells Bo:

"You need not apologize to me, Bo. I love you, son, and am so glad you are home safe. Now, let's get you where you belong.... home with your family!"

The servants want to aid Bo, but Amiel does not let them. He motions them to let him be. He wants to be the one taking him the rest of the way to the house. Amiel holds him around the waist to help him take some of the weight off his aching feet. Looking down at them makes Amiel cry. Just the thought that his boy is hurting so badly, cuts him to the heart. He also takes his right hand in his own.... just to touch the hand he'd held so often when he was a boy.

Amiel and the girls help Bo toward the house.

Bo speaks again:
"Father, I'm not even worthy to enter your house. How can you forgive me for what I've done?"

His father responds:
"Bo, you must understand that you coming back home, has filled a very large hole in my heart! Something inside of me died when you left. When I saw you again, that hole was instantly healed and that dead part of me came alive again! I am a very happy man!"

Amiel tells some of the servants who had followed him to meet Bo:
"Bring me the finest robe in the house, put it on my son, put a ring on his hand and shoes on his feet! Also kill the fatted calf and prepare it so that we can celebrate – to eat and be merry! For this son of mine was dead, and is alive again. He was lost, and now is found."

Amiel kisses his boy on the cheek, hugs him and then guides him into the house, where his sisters went to prepare a bath for him and lay out clean clothes so he can be ready for the celebration! While the servants process the fatted calf for the celebration, Bo now clean, is left to rest in his old room and bed. Amiel sends word out to his family and extended family who share the land to come and celebrate Bo's return. Once everything is ready, they celebrate with music, dancing, food and drink.

AMON ANGERED

Amon, the oldest son is out in one of the fields. When work is done, he makes his way to the house. He hears the music and sees people dancing. He thinks it odd! He doesn't know anything about a party or celebration. He wonders: "What is going on?" He asks one of the servants why there is a celebration?

The servant answers:

"Bo has returned and your fathered ordered a celebration in his honor!"

Amon becomes very angry and will not join the rest. The servant comes to Amiel and tells him how angry Amon is and that he will not come in. Amiel comes out to talk to him and to convince him to come join his family and friends.

He will not. Instead, he lets his father have it:

"All these years I've been faithful to you, served you, and never sinned against your authority and you never gave me a kid so I could celebrate with my friends! But as soon as this son of yours comes home, the one who devoured your living (wealth) with harlots... you kill a fatted calf for him!"

Amiel is very saddened that Amon feels this way. He takes him by the shoulders so he can be face to face with him.

He looks right into Amon's eyes with tears welling and says:

"Son, you are always with me, and all that I have is yours. It was fitting that we celebrate and be glad because your brother was dead and is alive again; he was lost and is found! Would you deny your father this feeling of great joy at your brother's return? I love you both equally. You, I've loved the longest. I will always have loved you the longest – to the day I die. Now, come and rejoice with me! That would make me doubly happy—to have both of my sons together again."

Amiel draws Amon to himself, hugs him, and weeps.

Amon is moved by his father's words and hug. He understands what his father is feeling. He apologizes for hurting him that way and says that he will clean up and join them in a short while.

Amon goes in the house where he can clean up and get a change of clothes, then, goes out where everyone is gathered. It is interesting when Amon enters the hall that a hush comes over the place. Everyone knew about Amon's great displeasure over Bo's decision to leave. They heard Amon repeat that displeasure many times as the weeks and months of Bo's absence turned into years, and how angry he was. But now, it was time to see if the grudge was still there.

Amon sees him sitting in a comfortable chair, his feet elevated with bandages, and dressed in some of the best clothes in the house. For a moment, he is disturbed but then he looks at Bo's face, emaciated and drawn, wearing half a smile as their eyes meet. Amon knows his brother is afraid of what he might say to him. To Amon, it's not the same Bo... he looks so beaten, defeated and worn. That brotherly love takes over and he approaches him with tears welling up in his eyes. As he gets to where Bo is sitting, Bo tries to get up in respect for his older brother.

Amon says to him:
"Don't get up, Bo! Stay seated. I've missed you, and I'm so glad to see you! I thank God that my little brother is home safe and sound. I too, was saddened when you left and I had an emptiness in my heart. I was angry with you but the sight of you brings me joy and has filled that void, as it has for our father. Welcome home Bo. I love you."

Bo returns the hug and kisses Amon's cheek. He asks his forgiveness for letting him down and abandoning the family. He tells Amon that he never forgot him, nor the things he taught him.

He adds:
"I love you too Amon."

Amon smiles and responds:
"Bo, I forgive you and I know that our relationship will be even stronger now. We will pick up where we left off before your trip. Now, enjoy the celebration and get your strength back."

With that, Amon bends over and hugs him with all his might and kisses his cheek again. Their father is watching all this and begins to weep with joy. He was afraid Amon would not accept him, but he is overjoyed with what he saw happening. He approaches them, squats down and hugs them both.

He then gets up and says:

"Everyone raise your cups and toast my two sons for the great joy they are to me. And ... raise them again to praise Adonai, Eloheinu (The Lord, our God) for His great mercies! L'Chayim"(to life.)"

After the celebration and years thereafter, Amiel, Amon, Bo, Ruth and Ana enjoy a pleasant and prosperous life. Bo marries, has three children and works his father's estate along with his brother Amon. Ruth and Ana also marry and have children. Eventually, Amiel dies peacefully at a ripe old age of eighty years of age He dies a very happy man!

THE END

Appendix

The Widow's Mite is the ancient small bronze lepton Biblical coin that was placed into the Temple offering box by the poor widow, who gave her last two coins. Mark 12:41-44 and Luke 21:1-4

* * *

HAND WASHING RITUAL .....NETILAT YADAYIM SHACHARIT

("Raising [after ritually washing] the hands of the morning"), when getting up in the morning after a full night's sleep, or even after a lengthy nap.

There is the custom to wash one's hands ritually by pouring a large cup of water over one's hands, alternating three times.

Prayer Tracey R. Rich ©copyright 5756-5771 (1995-2011)

After Kiddush (blessing) and before the meal, each person in the household should wash hands by filling a cup with water and pouring it over the top and bottom of the right hand and then the left hand. Before wiping the hands dry on a towel, the following blessing should be recited.

Barukh atah Adonai, Eloheinu, melekh ha-olam
Blessed are You, Lord, our God, King of the Universe

* * *

asher kidishanu b'mitz'votav v'tzivanu
Who has sanctified us with His commandments and commanded us

* * *

al n'tilat yadayim.
concerning washing of hands.

Shelters

The biblical customs concerning how a person should treat travelers and temporary residents were much different. They were more than simply ways to be polite or friendly, and went beyond entertaining guests. Hospitality customs were a vital part of the culture of the ancient world. *The people followed these customs as formal, even sacred, codes of conduct.*

Hospitality customs in the biblical world related to two distinct classes of people: the traveler and the resident alien. In most translations of the Bible, there is little attempt to try to separate the two. Even in the original Hebrew and Greek, different words are sometimes used interchangeably for the two groups. Either is called a stranger, one who does not belong to a particular community or group. Other terms applied to either or both are: foreigner, alien, sojourner, wayfarer, or gentile. In Israel, the law protected the resident alien, a foreigner who had settled permanently in the land. He could not own land, but he could participate in communal activities. The traveler, however, was extremely vulnerable. Only the force of the customs of hospitality protected him.

THE SABBATH/SHABBAT TABLE

The Sabbath table should be set with at least two candles (representing the dual commandments to remember and observe the Sabbath), a glass of wine, and at least two loaves of challah (representing the dual portion of manna that God provided for the Israelites in preparation for Shabbat in the desert). The challah loaves should be whole, and should be covered with a bread cover, towel or napkin.

LIGHTING CANDLES

Candles should be lit no later than 18 minutes before sundown. The two candles representing the dual commandments to remember and to keep the Sabbath. He covers his eyes, so as not to see the candles before reciting the blessing, and recites the blessing.

THE MEZUZAH

It's a widespread custom to kiss the mezuzah when leaving home, but once is probably enough. Actually, the custom is to touch the mezuzah with your hand and then kiss your hand. The Shulchan Aruch[1] mentions the custom to touch the mezuzah and to pray for Hashem to watch over you.

Hashem (another name for G-d)

Two inscriptions are to be written on parchment paper and placed on the back of the mezuzah.

Shaddai = God. serves as an acronym for:

Shomer Daltot Yisrael (Guardian of Israel's door)

Adonai, Eloheinu, Adonai (The Lord, our God, the Lord)

---

1   Shulchan Aruch: authoratative code of Jewish law and custom

About the author.... Roger Roberge Rainville

The author is the fifth oldest in a family of ten [French-speaking] children who was born in Magog, Québec, Canada on November 17, 1946. He is married and the proud father of two grown children; Linette and Christian. Both are in ministry.

When he was 8 years old, his family moved from Québec to Welland, Ontario where he learned to speak English before moving on to the Buffalo, New York area in April of 1959.

Roger was not a very good student in grade school or high school. At the age of thirty-eight, he went to college. Then, he turned on his brain and earned a bachelor's and master' degree to become a high school and college French and Spanish teacher. He suffered from ADD, and to a certain degree, dyslexia. With incredible effort, he managed to graduate "summa cum laude" for his Masters' degree.

Starting karate in 1969, he came to achieve the highest rank in his style of karate - 7th degree black belt – in Isshin-Ryu, and has promoted over twenty black belts.

He's a singer/guitar player and has had one of his original Christian songs recorded by a female gospel singer by the name of Jackie Davis. He rides a motor cycle and has been part of three Christian motorcycle ministries. Roger has done extensive street ministry among bikers and just as much, with prison inmates since 1981.

He is now retired and devoting much of his time to family, grand-children, friends, singing, riding his motorcycle, writing and, promoting Jesus wherever and whenever he can.

www.ingramcontent.com/pod-product-compliance
Lightning Source LLC
Chambersburg PA
CBHW060235180626
46813CB00007B/3088